Christina

Centau

pages is a frequency of support + guidance for you.

Following Bliss

Allow yourself to be opened to this expanded understanding that is here for you + know that

HEATHER STRANG

your bliss lies within you for your discovery.

xo
Heather
+ the fees

Copyright © 2013 by Heather Strang

License Notes: This book is for your personal enjoyment only. This book may not be re-sold. If you would like to share, please purchase an additional copy for each recipient. If you are reading this book and it was not purchased for your personal use, please purchase your own copy. Thank you for respecting and supporting the hard work of authors everywhere and allowing the book community to ever expand!

This book is a work of fiction. Names, characters, and incidents are products of the author's imagination or used fictitiously. Any resemblance to actual events or persons (living or dead) is entirely coincidental.

Cover art by Jim Thomson: http://jimkirkthomson.com

Visit Heather Strang at: HeatherStrang.com to learn more about her offerings.

Also, find her on Facebook at:
https://www.facebook.com/HeatherStrang11, visit her on Twitter: https://twitter.com/hkstrang or follow her on Pinterest https://www.pinterest.com/hkstrang/

"There is no ending to that which you are."

"You must understand how intricately involved everyone who is non-physical still is…You are about to remember who you really are and how we all fit together. And when you do, then you will be having a lot more fun."
—Esther Hicks from February 28, 2013

"When all your desires are distilled; You will cast just two votes: To love more, and be happy." —Hafiz

For Grandpa Earl. Who showed me explicitly that there is life after death and that it is filled with so much more love than we can imagine. Thank you, Grandpa, for being one of my guides on this path. xo

PROLOGUE

It wasn't that long ago that 38-year-old Daniel Tillman believed in love.

Well, if you consider time a relative concept that is. Eleven years ago, Daniel had known love. But then she left, taking his heart with her. And now here he was, broken-hearted and barely knowing what to do with himself. His mind lingered on thoughts of her, only to be pushed away by the insistence that he was merely a fool. If only he could do what she had wanted all along, if only he could find a way to show her how sorry he was and how much he loved her—then he was sure his life would be better. For now, he was as stuck as stuck could be.

Daniel attempted to pull himself out of his self-induced haze. He had to find a way to motivate himself out of stuckness and into action.

It's useless to think about her now. She's gone, there's nothing you can do.

Daniel scolded himself harshly, crumpling and tossing yet another page of meaningless words into the trash.

How in the world am I ever going to become a world famous novelist when I can't even finish one single page?

Daniel felt hopeless. His writing career, much like the rest of his life, was going nowhere.

Brushing his hand through his dark brown, stick-straight

hair, Daniel sighed loudly, his usually bright blue eyes a muted hue. There was no one to hear him, of course. The studio he had been renting out for the past year in Portland, Oregon's West Hills—in hopes of writing a great novel—had kept him pretty isolated. He imagined he liked it better that way, and found himself leaving the studio less and less, holing up instead to read more Steinbeck, fantasizing about what it would be like to be known for his words. Along with what it would be like if she hadn't left. Of course, he then had to remind himself that she had done the best she could; he had simply let it all fall apart. Now was his chance to redeem himself, to regain some of what he lost. But, his efforts seemed to be in vain.

Focus Daniel. Stop going over and over what you already know. She's gone. You're paying rent on this place and getting nothing done, and the time is now, or soon you'll be out on the street.

Daniel stood up, grabbed his favorite coffee mug, the one with "I heart Portland" written on it, and walked into his small kitchenette. Dirty dishes laid in the sink, along with a half-eaten pizza from Pizzicato on the countertop. With only him living in the studio, he hadn't put much effort into decorating. A "Kiss the Cook" apron hung on a hook, but he rarely took the time to whip up anything more than soup and salads. And looking down at what he was wearing, Daniel realized his lack of decoration or effort in his studio also reflected how he was taking care of himself. He hadn't bothered putting on more than workout pants and a white T-shirt, along with his favorite Adidas flip-flops—this had quickly become his outfit of choice as a writer. At 5'11" and 175 pounds, Daniel could pull it off. He found regular visits to the Pearl Districts' LA Fitness helped work off the frustration and angst he had been feeling (along with giving him a rock solid six-pack), regularly spending time sitting in the steam room, imagining the block to writing his great novel being released from his pores. Daniel sighed again, letting the breath slowly move out of him, while pouring himself yet another cup of decaf (although he wouldn't dare admit this to anyone—Portland was known for its stellar coffee after all), but the caffeine buzz was too strong for Daniel. It only exacerbated his anxiety and panic about the life he wanted to create, but seemed incapable of doing anything about. He took a long, slow sip out of the steaming cup. He was stalling and he knew it.

It was a gray and cloudy Tuesday in early September. Daniel looked out the window, noticing a patch of blue sky off in the distance. The weatherman had said the clouds would burn off and Daniel wasn't sure if that was a good thing or not. Fall in Portland was always his favorite time of year, with warm temps, sunny skies and cool nights. The gray made him want to curl up and sleep, but the sun made him want to get outside. Neither was helpful for his writing career. And while he had bits and pieces of his historical novel written, it wasn't nearly enough to present at this weekend's annual Willamette Writers Conference. He didn't even have enough to show a literary agent. He had given himself this week as a deadline, hoping it would summon forth inspiration and a sense of urgency. It hadn't.

He took another swig of his coffee as his mind pondered his remaining options.

Option 1: Bail on the conference all together and go back to working in radio.

Daniel laughed at the thought of this. He had spent 10 years working in morning radio in small- to mid-sized markets all over the country. It had taken a lot of courage to leave it last year to pursue his passion as a writer. He had made some cash here and there writing for publications, but mostly he lived off of the money he had saved while working in radio—taking every additional gig he could. Truth be told, he hated those weekend gigs—whether it was a car show, an air show or a furniture store's grand opening—but he knew it was all for the greater good of supporting his career as an author.

It wasn't that he hated radio. And he was actually really good at it. His morning show always became number one in whatever market he worked in, and he usually obtained a solid following of listeners who would come out to whatever BBQ, grand opening or public event he was emceeing. He had even done some local dating events and pseudo-celebrity auctions, getting auctioned off on a "date" for charity one year. *Boy, was that a disaster,* he thought. The girl had been roughly 100 pounds of pure ditz and seemed more like a stalker than a supportive fan.

Even so, all those years hadn't been bad, it was just that his heart and soul wanted more. He hit a wall and knew if he didn't make a move soon, he would be 80 years old in no time and still not living his dream—to be a famous writer like his idol John Steinbeck. And then any hope of proving himself worthy of her love would be over.

So, while going back to radio on the surface seemed like an option, Daniel couldn't bring himself to do it—not yet anyway. He still had plenty of money in savings (and some that was doing quite well in an investment account he had created to grow his money further). He had made some small steps forward—publication in various journals, writing some book reviews and even being part of a short story anthology—and he wasn't about to give up, no matter how bleak his situation was looking on that Tuesday morning.

Option 2: Scrape together the bits of the book he had and put it together in proposal form, spending the rest of the week writing up a brilliant marketing plan (of which he had no idea how to do) and use that to woo the perfect agent for him. And he was pretty sure he knew who that was, but more obsessing would be done on that portion of the option later.

Option 3: (Quite possibly the least attractive of the options and certainly the most difficult.) No sleeping, and working round the clock to write a solid three chapters to present to the agent of his choice—Ms. Kaley Hamilton. She represented some of the best authors in the historical fiction world and, from what he read about her, she seemed to have the know-how and gumption to take a struggling, no-name writer and launch him/her into super-stardom. He had watched it happen with Garrett Lamphier. Garrett had met Kaley at a writing conference in Hawaii a few years back, with only a shoddy manuscript in tow. Kaley was so impressed that she worked tirelessly (as told by *Lit Lovers* magazine, that is) to create an amazing package that Penguin couldn't resist.

He had to impress her.

Damn it. How in the world am I going to pull this off?

But, he couldn't be deterred. This was his life's work; he was sure of it. He had to find a way to get it together before meeting Ms. Hamilton that weekend at the conference. Daniel grabbed his coffee mug, planted it firmly on his antique oak desk (if antique meant finding it on a street corner on Northeast Broadway with a "free" sign) and planted himself firmly in his seat. To write, he needed his butt in the chair and his laptop in front of him. Daniel had been browsing YouTube late one night when he came across Abraham-Hicks. In it, he had watched countless videos about the Law of Attraction and creating one's reality. He figured this was as good a time as any to apply these principles, especially when he was clearly at the stage in the process where he needed to take some action to show the Universe he was serious about all of this. It seemed as though his very life depended on it.

Just write, Daniel. You can do this.

And without warning, his fingers began typing, as though they had known all along what needed to be done. Daniel took a deep breath and smiled.

―――

"Excuse me Miss, Miss—your order is ready."

The bakery assistant at New Seasons Market was trying to get the young woman's attention.

Shelby Hanson looked up startled, her green eyes wide and brimming with tears, her wavy blonde hair tousled and messy. Her mind had been anywhere but where she was. She had been so out of sorts when she got up in the morning from a night of sleep filled with intense dreams (of which she could not make any sense out of just yet) that she had simply thrown on a black wrap dress, a scarf and her rain coat (the gray skies were slightly deceiving, given the forecast for sun and warm temps) barely taking time to do her hair or put on more than a coat of mascara and lip gloss. She took the cupcakes from the woman and smiled apologetically.

"Half a dozen gluten-free vanilla cupcakes with chocolate ganache frosting and sprinkles, all ready for you. What's the special occasion?"

Shelby couldn't help but feel grateful to the woman who was bringing her back to the present moment.

"Oh, just a surprise for my little sister. She passed a major exam this week and I wanted to do something special for her. She's gluten intolerant, so doesn't have enough cupcakes in her life." Shelby giggled slightly.

Her sister Laney who was 24 to Shelby's 29 probably couldn't care less about cupcakes, but Shelby loved nurturing people with food, so she was always picking up treats for her. They had three other sisters who lived on the Oregon Coast, but since they lived so far away, Laney received the majority of Shelby's need to nurture. Besides, whatever Laney didn't eat could go to her housemates. Laney was an urban hippie, living in a large home with a few other people—Shelby could never keep track of them—there was always someone moving in or out. In many ways she admired Laney. She didn't work at a job, she was finishing her certification as a Cranial-Sacral practitioner (hence the cupcakes) and "manifested" money (her words) whenever she needed it. The rest she traded—sessions for local produce, haircuts, clothes, other healing work, etc. She was constantly telling Shelby to relax and "go with the flow."

And as attractive as "going with the flow" was to Shelby, she didn't quite have it down. She worried about money and felt she needed to "do" work in order to "manifest" it. The thought of waking up every day not knowing where the next dollar was coming from or how she'd pay rent terrified her. But, not having to deal with her crazy editor boss to "manifest" that money might be really wonderful, too. She couldn't decide the lesser of the two evils.

Shelby worked for Portland's premier magazine, *Hello Portland,* and her editor, Dillion Turkin, was true to stereotypical form. As an assistant staff writer, Shelby was at Dillion's mercy. He often sent her on coffee runs and demanded she take on other menial tasks (one time she even had to fetch toilet paper for the staff bathrooms!). He never returned her email requests and always made her wait until the last second before letting her know when her stories would be featured in the magazine. And he was notorious for asking her two days before an issue had to go to press for last-minute photos, details and interview questions. She was constantly on edge, never knowing what he would throw at her. She felt like he was often working against her. And despite her best attempts—she had invited him to her birthday party the past two years and he never so much as even responded to her invites—he seemed to not even know she existed outside of what she could do for him.

On her way to pick up Laney's cupcakes for tonight, Dillion had called her, asking that she get a few more quotes from her most recent piece about an international flight attendant who was based in Portland. The issue was set to go to press in two days and the woman was unavailable traveling—a fact she had shared with Dillion three weeks ago when she submitted the story, and again the following week when she asked if he needed anything further. And that's why she had been so grateful that the bakery woman's question had brought her back to the present moment. She was feeling totally helpless after Dillion's last request. She had no idea how she was going to pull it all off and still get to Laney's celebration. Shelby was at her breaking point—tumultuous sleep and Dillion's most recent pressure-filled demand was pushing her too far.

Working for an un-organized, passive-aggressive, detached editor only made Shelby want to give it all up to pursue her true passion—jewelry. Shelby had been making jewelry ever since she could remember, giving her designs as gifts and fending off requests from family and friends to make more. Her job at *Hello Portland* was supposed to simply pay the bills while she grew her jewelry business. But, that never seemed to happen, as the demands of the job and her crazy editor took up more time than she expected. And when she was free, she was so exhausted that designing jewelry was the last thing on her mind.

Shelby sent Laney a quick "pick-me-up" text.

Got u some celebration goodies. Altho may consume it all due 2 my cray cray editor. Excited 2 hang w-u! Xo

Laney didn't take long to reply. She was always good like that when it came to Shelby. Since they were the only two sisters living in the city, they agreed they had to look out for each other.

Honor the flo sis. Besides, all ed r cray cray. Don't sweat it. Mayb time 2 bring ur jewelry 2 the world? Love u! xo

Shelby had to laugh. Laney was right, crazy editors were par for the course in the writing world. Complaining about her boss and allowing him to ruin her day was just making her a stereotypical staff writer. Laughing—even to herself—eased her tension and she felt lighter. Her blonde, shoulder-length hair bounced as she picked up her stride, making her way out to her blue Acura TSX, cupcakes in hand. Besides, she was only 29 years old; this wasn't going to be her life forever. She had big plans. Plans to be a successful jewelry designer. Plans that not even Dillion Turkin and his ridiculous requests could deter.

1

Daniel stood at the entrance of the Willamette Writers Conference feeling two things—fear and excitement. He had taken Option C, working non-stop since Tuesday, and felt both giddy by what had been created and fearful that Ms. Kaley Hamilton would tear it to pieces once she read it. That was the problem with being a writer, Daniel thought, all you can think about is writing and then when you do write, all you can think about is whether people will like it or not.

Even so, something had come over him for the past few days in such an intense way that he could almost say he didn't write the novel that was in his hands now. He had read a few books on the Law of Attraction (which says that like attracts like) and felt like he had some kind of surrender moment. Like all the intensity of having to complete the manuscript and show it to Kaley became so overwhelming that he had no choice but to surrender. And when he did, it was as if some other power or force had flowed through him. While he had a few brief moments of stuck-ness, all in all things flowed, and now in his hands was his completed historical novel, *Shannon Town*. His goal had been to get the first three chapters solid, but instead he took his outline with a few paragraphs for each chapter written and completed the entire story.

It was like some magical Law of Attraction meets surrender spell had been cast on him and it allowed him to write more easily than before. Almost as though he was meant to write this book, no matter what.

Well, here I am. And here it is. Daniel took a deep breath. *Let's do this.*

Daniel checked his registration. He wasn't set to meet with Ms. Hamilton until 12:30 p.m. He had a lecture to attend before that—giving him some time to settle into the atmosphere of the conference before having to give the performance of a lifetime to one of the best literary agents for his genre.

Daniel chuckled. At least he wasn't putting any pressure on himself. This was ironic, of course, because all he ever did was put pressure on himself. As an only child, Daniel felt tremendous pressure to be his parents' "everything," and so ever since he could remember, he was always pushing himself to do more and then berating himself for not doing it perfectly.

Oh wait, Daniel remembered, *that was my dad pushing and then berating me, I just picked up where he left off.* He sighed, internally getting himself back on track. *Save that for therapy, Daniel, you are here on a mission to launch your career as a historical fiction author. The berating can wait.*

Daniel checked the room number for his first lecture on character development, which was taking place in the St. Helens room at the Sheraton Hotel at the Portland Airport. All of the rooms were given Portland-esque names. Clever, Daniel thought, as he meandered his way through the conference halls, dodging writers who had come from all over the state and the West Coast to attend the conference. The energy throughout the hotel was somber as many, like Daniel, knew they would only have a couple of shots (or one) at this year's conference to garner the attention of a powerful agent or publisher. People were speaking in hushed tones, clinging to their binders and bags, which possibly contained the world's next great book. Daniel couldn't help but strain his ears a time or two to overhear a few conversations as he passed people in the halls.

"You know, everyone is saying eBooks are the wave of the future. Soon we won't even need hard copy books."

Daniel couldn't imagine a world without libraries and bookstores, or not being able to curl up on the couch with a book in his hands, feeling the pages between his fingers. But, he also knew that the tides were shifting and with e-readers, iPads and larger than life smartphones, anything was possible. Besides, the format of the work didn't really matter—what mattered was getting his words and his message to as many people as possible.

"He said not to waste my time. That there are thousands of other young adult novelists out there trying to make it after J.K. Rowling's success."

That woman had already met with an agent, and he told her not to waste her time? Yikes. Daniel could only hope Kaley Hamilton would be more gentle with him.

Daniel realized he had circled the conference area twice now. He had been so captivated by the people-watching and eavesdropping that he had yet to find his lecture. Just then he walked by two men huddled together and overhead:

"Yeah, they say some of the agents are going incognito and sitting in on lectures to scope out authors ahead of time."

Daniel froze.

She wouldn't.

Would she?

Kaley Hamilton probably hadn't become the best agent in her genre by playing by the rules. Daniel wished he would have paid more attention to her photo beforehand. He would have no idea if she was in the room. Suddenly, his khaki pants and white polo seemed insufficient for making the right first impression with an agent as accomplished as Kaley Hamilton. He looked down at his messenger bag with his manuscript. And what if she laughed when she heard his pitch? He imagined Kaley Hamilton dressed in white silk, looking down at him, asking that he not waste his and the rest of the world's time writing historical fiction.

Beads of sweat began forming on Daniel's forehead. He swallowed hard, clenched his fists, took a deep breath and turned back around. He was going to have to get it together (and possibly Google Kaley Hamilton's picture) before he could walk into that lecture.

As Daniel made a bee-line for the restroom to search Google on his smartphone, he locked eyes with an old writing friend, Gregory LaTour.

"Hey Gregory! Long time, how are you doing?"

"Daniel, it's so great to see you here. Seems as though we're both still living the writer's dream, eh?"

Daniel chuckled. Gregory was in his mid-sixties and after retiring from a long career as an electrician, he was now pursuing his desire to write novels about World War I and II, two of his long-time passions. Daniel had met Gregory at a Powell's Books writing group two winters ago.

"Yes, most definitely living the dream, Gregory, although I'm hoping to create a much better dream here shortly. Are you still involved with the writing group?" Daniel inquired, as he wiped his forehead. He hoped Gregory didn't notice how nervous he was.

"Nah, I left it shortly after you did. I felt like it was a lot of ego-stroking and competition, and way too much coffee drinking. I had to give up caffeine, and decaf just didn't taste as good," Gregory laughed.

"Didn't you have to give up smoking too? What's left?" Daniel always enjoyed Gregory's outlook on life, always the optimist and jokester. He felt himself beginning to relax as he focused more on Gregory and less on the nervous tension he had been feeling.

Gregory nodded. "Yep, giving up the bad stuff so I can enjoy more of the good stuff, like writing. Speaking of, I just ran into a few friends who did pitches already this morning. One got in with that historical fiction gal, you know her, Kaley Hamilton. I guess she's a real spitfire, but totally harmless. In fact, my friend Cal and she hit it off grandly. Cal isn't sure if she'll represent his work, but said they had a blast chatting about writing and their love of historical fiction. Who knew? I thought all those fancy pants agents were a little stuck up. Have you met with anyone yet?"

"Gregory, god bless you. I meet with Kaley later on today and I was starting to get nervous. I heard some agents were even sneaking in on lectures to scope authors out. I wasn't sure if I was going to be able to go into my lecture, I was so worried about running into her and making the wrong impression."

"Oh yeah, I heard about that, too. But really, who cares? If it's meant to happen, it's gonna happen. I'm just glad to hear there are some nice ones out there. Well, I better be going—good to see you again, Daniel."

Gregory gave him a hug and went on his way.

Daniel couldn't help but smile. Not only was it odd to run into Gregory after not seeing him in so long, but for him to mention the same agent Daniel was worried about seeing and to give her a glowing review—well, that was exactly the kind of magic Daniel was hoping for. And it was most definitely the reminder Daniel needed.

He turned right back around and headed for the lecture. Whether Kaley Hamilton was spying on authors or not, he suddenly didn't care to know. His confidence had returned from the interaction with Gregory.

As Daniel walked up to the lecture door, he felt his nervous energy rise again. Only this time it was feeling nervous that she *wouldn't* be there. After talking with Gregory, Daniel was reminded that the Universe was looking out for him, and now he felt ready to see Kaley, and impress her so much she would offer to be his agent right there on the spot.

The conference room was pretty full, with about 100 people jammed into the room. Daniel found a spot along the wall to stand, and then began scoping out who was in attendance. As he gazed over the crowd of people, a blonde woman caught his eye. She was talking to someone else, but something about her pulled his attention in. He couldn't stop looking at her. Her eyes caught his gaze and she gave him a half smile. Daniel felt as if an electrical cord was connecting them together.

"Welcome to 'Character Development for All Genres.'"

A woman's voice echoed across the room. Daniel had brought a notebook and pen to take notes for the conference lectures, but something about the blonde woman across the room made it very difficult to focus. He kept trying to re-center himself and pay attention, but it was almost like the electrical zap he felt from her kept pulling his attention over to her.

It made the lecture's 45 minutes seem like an eternity.

All Daniel knew was that as soon as it was over, he had to talk to that woman.

As the crowd began to leave the conference room, Daniel attempted to make his way over to where the woman was. He didn't take his eyes off of her, sure that if he did she might vanish and he would never see her again. He noticed though, that for whatever reason, she was staying put, saying good-bye to a few folks, but not leaving the room. Maybe she had felt the electrical zing as well.

When he finally made his way over to her, she was talking with someone that she seemed to know rather well, so Daniel stood off to the side while staying in her peripheral vision. She looked over at him and smiled. He took this as a good sign. She said her good-byes and turned to face him.

"Well hello," she said, grinning from ear to ear.

"Hello," Daniel said, matching her smile.

"We seem to have noticed each other even from clear across this crowded room," she said.

"We did. And I was intent on getting over here or I'd never forgive myself. So, thank you for not leaving."

"Well, I have to confess, I had the same intention. I'm Shelby, by the way," she said, extending her hand to him.

"Shelby, great to meet you," Daniel said as he took her hand in his, shaking it lightly, but focusing more on the feel of her skin. "I'm Daniel. So...do you come here often?"

They both broke into laughter, relaxing more.

"Oh, all the time. I just *love* to hang out at the Sheraton Hotel. Such great ambiance, I find that it really inspires me." Shelby teased.

"Ah, I see. What sort of inspiration are we talking?"

"Yeah, well, let's see—I've already mentally written two fantastically successful feature pieces for *Hello Portland*, as well as designed a complete line of jewelry during my time here."

Daniel was enjoying their exchange. This Shelby, whomever she was, with her bright green eyes, luscious blonde hair, beautiful lips and delicious curves (yes, it was true, he had spent most of the conference finding ways to check her out), was also really fun. He couldn't help but hear a voice that whispered, *"And fun is exactly what you need right now Daniel."* He wasn't sure where the voice was coming from, but he was enjoying himself too much to care.

"Turns out, you are in great company, because I too am wildly successful. The proud author of a series of historical fiction novels…"

With the mention of his books, Kaley Hamilton and the pitch popped into Daniel's awareness.

"Oh wow, I am so sorry. I just realized I'm supposed to be pitching to an agent in like 10 minutes. Do you want to walk over to the agents' ballroom with me?"

Shelby smiled, happy he hadn't just ended the conversation, but wanted to spend some more time with her.

"So, you're also embellishing about your success right now?" she teased back. "Don't worry, in my current reality I'm a staff writer for *Hello Portland*, but my dream is to be a world-famous, or actually, I would settle for making an awesome living as a jewelry designer."

"Writing for *Hello Portland* isn't too shabby, Shelby. That's practically two steps away from jewelry super-stardom. And yes, I was embellishing a bit. I'm a writer working to have my first historical novel published. But someday, yes, someday it will be a series, a renowned series—it may even make it into the school library systems, to be read by future writers and book lovers everywhere."

Daniel added dramatic flair to his story taking his right arm and spreading it out and around as he described his high hopes for his novels. Shelby burst into laughter, covering her mouth with her hand.

"I'm so sorry! I'm not laughing at you, I swear. I love that you have a vision for what you want to create. You know, that's really important and it's the only way we create—by having the vision first."

"It's okay. I'm amping it up just a little for you," Daniel winked.

He didn't know what had gotten into him, but being around Shelby made him feel like a million bucks.

As they walked out of the conference room and toward the ballroom where the literary agents were, Daniel and Shelby kept looking at each other and smiling. When they arrived at the ballroom door where the agents were being sequestered, Daniel turned to her and Shelby heard a voice within her whisper, *"This guy."*

She was so taken aback by this whisper that she burst into laughter yet again and leaned into Daniel, giving him a big hug.

As they pulled back, Daniel looked into her eyes and said, "I have to see you again. You game?"

"Absolutely."

Shelby handed him her card and wished him luck. Daniel smiled to himself as she walked away, thinking, *with you coming into my life, luck is the last thing I need.*

And just like that, he walked into the ballroom, manuscript in hand to meet Ms. Kaley Hamilton.

2

Daniel was buzzing from his exchange with Shelby, so much so that it hardly occurred to him to be nervous about pitching his book to Kaley Hamilton. As he walked over to the table, he was radiating—his smile beaming from his face in a manner he could not contain. Kaley Hamilton took notice right away.

"I have no idea what your book is about, but I sure do love the positive energy emanating from you!"

She stood up, extending her hand. Daniel returned her handshake, noting how strong she was. In fact, he was pretty sure she might crush his hand. This was surprising as Kaley's petite 5'1" frame and brunette, slightly newscaster-ish-bob hairstyle could possibly indicate a slight, demure woman. But, Kaley was a woman who meant business—Daniel could feel it right away. Dressed to the nines in a charcoal gray Ann Taylor suit, complete with a chunky gold-and-black bracelet and a matching necklace, there was no way anyone could mistake Kaley Hamilton for anything other than smart and on top of her game. And her handshake? Well, it cleared things up in case there was any question. When it came to the literary arts, Ms. Hamilton was certainly in charge and in control.

"Thank you so much for taking the time to hear more about my book, Ms. Hamilton," Daniel said calmly, as he retracted his hand from her grip.

"Oh, please—call me Kaley." Kaley sat back down into her chair, crossing her legs and leaning one arm over the back of the chair, making sure Daniel had the opportunity to notice her rather short, mid-thigh length skirt. Kaley smiled pleasingly at Daniel as she said, "Now tell me, what kind of book are *you* going to share with the world?"

Daniel went on to articulately and confidently outline to Ms. Hamilton—er, Kaley—the scope of his novel, its relevance to readers, and the best ways to reach his market. He felt like he was on top of the world. Never, in all of his faux practice sessions, had he spoken so eloquently about what his message was and what he wanted the world to know through his books. Kaley sat captivated, nodding in approval and smiling at him as he spoke. When he finished, he took a deep breath and paused. Kaley interjected.

"Well Daniel, that is quite the presentation. As I'm sure you may know, Western historical fiction has been on the decline for some time now, and it's not something publishers are generally jumping up and down for. But, I've got to tell you, I like your energy and if that's shining through in your novel, then we just might have a winner."

Daniel felt a lump form in his throat, hoping his novel was as fantastic as he had made it sound. *If only I had met Shelby last week—if this energy was embedded in the manuscript, I wouldn't be able to go wrong.*

"I'll tell you what," Kaley continued. "I want to take the next few days to read over your manuscript and see how it feels to me. Then, I'll email you and we can discuss next steps. If you don't hear from me by Wednesday, feel free to reach out to me directly." She handed him her card. "My assistant, Sarah, usually responds to this email address, but I'll let her know to forward yours to me. Sound good?"

Daniel could hardly believe his ears. Kaley Hamilton was going to make sure his emails made it directly to her? He said a silent thank you to the Universe for this incredible turn of events. It was as if someone else was orchestrating things for him. From the moment he made the decision to go for it and make the pitch to Kaley with a completed manuscript, everything fell into place—being able to complete his novel fully in a week's time (even as a rough draft, this was a big accomplishment for him), meeting up with Gregory right at the perfect moment to be assured Kaley wasn't some rabid agent, walking into the lecture hall and instantly seeing Shelby, having such a powerful connection with her that he forgot to be nervous to meet Kaley, and that allowed him to deliver the best pitch of his life. Daniel felt blessed. He didn't know how his luck had so suddenly changed, but he wasn't complaining.

"Kaley, that sounds perfect. I'm confident you're going to love this story as much as I do, and as much as readers will."

Who was this guy that made sweeping gestures to attractive women he had only recently met and claimed complete confidence in his writing? He wasn't sure, but he was loving this new version of himself— that had apparently been birthed when he met Shelby.

Kaley stood up, extending her hand once again. "Thank you, Daniel. It was a pleasure. And whatever it is that you're doing to radiate this kind of energy, please keep it up. The world needs more of it."

Daniel smiled, shook her hand—noticing this time that it was a lot less crushing and said, "You've got it, Kaley. I look forward to speaking with you next week."

And while Daniel couldn't fully comprehend how beautifully things were unfolding, he felt a sense of calm and ease, along with a knowing that all was exactly as it was meant to be.

———

Shelby walked away from Daniel in a state of ecstasy. She couldn't believe the amount of electricity she felt in her body while they were talking. It was as if some type of electrical current system was zigzagging throughout her entire body. It was so intense, focusing on the content of their conversation was nearly impossible. And he wanted to see her again! Shelby felt giddy at the possibility of getting to know Daniel better. Now, the trick was not to sit around and stew about when he would call and what would happen next. She knew that by worrying about the details, she would be energetically pushing away what she wanted.

Laney had turned her onto that insight—and Shelby had experienced it time and time again. Whenever she needed something to happen, it didn't seem to happen *or* it took forever to come to fruition. When she didn't care much or was able to trust it would work out the way it was meant to, things seemed to happen right away. A fact was a fact and Shelby knew it—people/places/things flowed into her experience more rapidly when she detached from needing it to happen.

But, even so, she made sure her phone volume was on high—at all times.

That night her friend Kathryn called—they had met several months ago at a healing circle facilitated by healer and intuitive Derrick Milestone. Laney had insisted that Shelby check it out, reminding her that if she wanted to run her jewelry business full-time and eventually meet the love of her life, she was going to have to do some healing work.

"Listen Shelb, I love you. But sitting around making pros-and-cons lists and mentally trying to willpower your new life into fruition is not going to work," Laney had said, sounding almost like their mother, who was known for her killer ability to scold just about anyone.

"It's not?" Shelby had stared over at her blankly as the two speed-walked their way from OMSI to Sellwood and back on the Springwater Corridor.

Laney squealed. "And who's the older sister here? You can't force things to happen. You need to clear whatever blocks are keeping you from having what you want. Willpower is soooo 2008, by the way. It's 2013, get with the program," with that Laney had sprinted up ahead of Shelby, leaving her with the distinct feeling that Laney—although her younger sis—was far wiser than Shelby at times.

Shelby had spent her life strong-arming her way through.

She literally will-powered her way through workouts, job interviews, dating—even grocery shopping. What if she relaxed a bit and let the Universe take the wheel? She decided that it was time to give some of Laney's woo-woo-ness a try.

Before she knew it, she was sitting in the metaphysical bookstore Healing Waters & Sacred Spaces receiving energy healing work from Derrick. Sitting next to her was Kathryn, a lovely woman with curly brown locks, an infectious smile and sparkling blue eyes. The two started chatting during a break, bonding over their mutual love of macaroons and consignment shopping.

Kathryn had recently come together with her true love, Scott, and Shelby loved her conversations with Kathryn about love and all of the possibilities of the Universe. Up until Kathryn, Shelby had only Laney to talk to about mystical occurrences in her life. Now, that's all she and Kathryn did, preferably while eating macaroons, of course. Shelby had to give massive props to Laney for telling her about Derrick's healing circle. Although a newbie to the new thought community, she was enjoying playing with the concept of the Law of Attraction and working more deliberately with non-physical energy.

And so, as soon as she heard Kathryn's voice on the other end of the line the evening after the writer's conference, she blurted out, "Kathryn, you'll never believe what happened today. I think I met the guy. In fact, when I met him, I heard a voice that said, "This is the guy." I have never had *that* happen!"

"OMG Shelby, this is soooo exciting. Do you think he felt it too?" Kathryn inquired with almost the same level of intensity Shelby was feeling.

"I'm pretty sure, he was beaming the entire time we spoke and said he had to see me again. So...I'm taking that as a sign that we're on the right track."

"Love it! And I love that you are so open to what's happening. I wish I would have been more open with Scott. As you know, when I met him, he felt it right away, but I was too busy chasing some dude around that had the same name and occupation that a psychic had given me several months back. God, I was so unbelievably lame back then," Kathryn laughed.

Kathryn had shared with Shelby that she had spent a lot of time questing for her true love, but was subconsciously sabotaging and pushing it away. Shelby had been very lucky in love throughout her life, always attracting wonderful men, but never feeling the spark that made her want to commit. And while she wanted children, she was only 29 years old and didn't feel any need to force things. She had always felt like that part of her life would work itself out. She had never struggled to have a relationship and Laney assured her this was based on her strong belief system that it would be effortless, and so it was. Apparently, what one believes always manifests into their physical reality. Laney made sure to repeat this message to Shelby whenever she had the chance.

"This is how the Universe works Shelby, get on board, apply the same principles you do with men and relationships to your career and you'll have the same blessings!" Laney had often reminded her.

Somehow, when it came to the Universe, Laney always had the answers. And as hard as it was sometimes to admit, from what Shelby was learning, Laney was right. She always assumed she would meet the perfect guy for her when the time was right and, as a byproduct, they would get married and have babies. But, it certainly wasn't something she worried about. Her career, on the other hand, was something she was always trying to "figure out." And no matter what she did, it seemed like she always ended up in the same place—at a job she hated while subsequently spending most of her time busying herself with meaningless tasks and dreaming about leaving.

Hearing Kathryn and Scott's true love story caused Shelby to think about more about the kind of *life* she wanted—not merely focusing on her career or feeling passive about love. From what she was learning, if she wanted the life of her dreams, she needed to be intentional about her desires. *All her desires.* Segmenting life into blocks of focus wasn't necessarily the best way to manifest. Everything worked together as a whole. And the more she got to know Kathryn, the more she realized that a true love partnership had the ability to allow one to grow in ways you couldn't grow on your own. That by deeply loving, the other parts of one's life also expanded and grew. As an example, Kathryn had not been interested in having children before meeting Scott, but through the depth of their connection, she realized there was deep healing work that needed to be done around this area of her life. She had embarked on a healing journey, and now she and Scott were talking about the possibility of having children—after their commitment ceremony, that was. They were also finding ways to create a unique partnership that didn't fall into the usual paradigms of relationship in the Western world.

To Shelby, it was a sign that anything was possible where love and life was concerned—no matter if you were questing for it or waiting to receive it. Now, in light of meeting Daniel, her intentionality for what she wanted in a romantic relationship was becoming clearer. Just meeting him made her want more...of him.

"But look how everything turned out Kathryn? You and Scott are planning your commitment ceremony and talking about having children—something you never thought you'd do. And for me, ever since that healing circle we went to several months ago, I feel lighter and I have more confidence that everything is always working out for me. I even bounce back from being triggered by my boss more quickly than before. It used to take me days of seething at Dillion before I felt back to normal. But, through my healing work and our friendship, everything is changing. And now Daniel. He was so very sweet, animated and really present, which I love. I gave him my card and now I'm doing everything I can to not stare at my phone until it rings."

They both laughed.

"Well, you know how the Universe works, so the second you stop looking at the phone and go do something else—he'll call," Kathryn reminded her.

"I know, I know. I've got to do something to distract myself."

"By the way, Scott and I are having a few friends over for dinner Friday night—you interested?"

"Yes, I would love to! What should I bring?"

"If you can, just bring some red wine. You know me with all my food allergies, so we'll have the food covered. You're such a lucky girl, you can eat whatever you want. Just don't bring any mac n' cheese to torture me with and we'll be fine."

"Deal. And you know I wouldn't taunt you with gluten and dairy—well, not at your own party anyway. For the wine, I'm presuming a good Malbec is in order?"

Kathryn was a known lover of the Argentine red wine.

"You know me well. Besides, I've got to enjoy as much of it as I can before we get pregnant. Speaking of…I better get going to bed. Scott is already there."

"You two are so adorable. Thanks so much for listening Kathryn. Sleep well and I'll talk to you soon. Oh, and send good thoughts about my guy."

"Oh, he's calling. As soon as you're away from your phone, that is."

―――

Go to him. Give him my message. He has to know the truth.

Shelby sat up in bed with a start, looking around. She could have sworn she heard a woman's voice.

You have to tell him to meditate, every day. He needs to do this. He needs to open up his heart. Only you can do this.

Shelby rubbed her eyes. She looked around her bedroom, but didn't see anyone. Just her white-washed nightstand, a vision board that she and Laney created one night while watching *The Bachelor* and drinking red wine (complete with all that she hoped to manifest in the next several years—a new jewelry station, a Canon Rebel, and a vacation to Paris, among other things) and her grandparents' maple TV stand that she converted into a dresser. Was she dreaming? She had been in a dead sleep and wasn't sure if the voice was happening in her dream or outside of her sleep state.

She lay back down, but as soon as she closed her eyes, she heard the voice again.

He needs you. You must give him this message.

"Who???" Shelby yelled out loud. She was a combination of freaked out and angry. No one messed with her sleep—not even non-physical beings from beyond or weird dreams within dreams, or whatever this was.

Silence. She didn't hear a thing.

"Oh, so now you don't have anything to say?? Thanks a lot. Who am I supposed to give this message to and why is it so important that you tell me at…" Shelby grabbed her cell phone off of the nightstand. "3:35 a.m.? You know what, if you want me to give a message to someone, you're going to have to do a better job than this at delivering it to me. How about sending me an email? That would be a lot more convenient!"

Shelby lay back down with a loud sigh. Waiting, wondering what the hell was going on. Nothing. Just dead, middle-of-the-night silence filled the air. But now, Shelby was so amped up that she couldn't go back to sleep. She laid there for some time before she finally felt the pull of sleep come over her.

At 8 a.m., Shelby's alarm (the lovely sounds of a cello) awoke her. She was thick with sleep, the images from a dream still hanging on. As she laid in bed, attempting to wake-up, the details of the dream became clearer. So clear, that Shelby was shocked at the content.

Daniel was there. He was in a garden, sitting on a park bench. He was smiling so handsomely that she wanted to run to him, jump into his arms and never leave—and possibly spend a lot of time making out with him while in those strong, sexy arms. But that wasn't the point of *this* dream. He was smiling at something off in the distance. Then, Shelby watched as a young woman and her small son walked by. Daniel was watching them. The woman stopped to help her son put on his jacket, and even Shelby—as the observer— felt a chill hit the air. The little boy put his arms around his mother and said, "I love you, mommy." Shelby watched as Daniel's eyes filled with tears. He slowly got up, and walked away. As he was walking away the woman turned to Shelby.

You have to tell him. Tell him I'm here and that it's time. It's time for him to open his heart. You are the only one that can do this Shelby.

Shelby looked at the woman more closely. She had brown, almost black hair, pinned back and was wearing a fitted navy dress, in the style you would see in the late 1950s—dressed somewhat like the perfect Stepford wife. Her brown eyes were dark, and the way she looked at Shelby made her feel very uncomfortable.

Why do I need to tell him? Why are you coming to me? Shelby asked in her dream state.

Because he'll listen to you, Shelby. Please. I've tried everything and I need your help.

The alarm had cut short the rest of the dream. Now that Shelby was more awake, the events of the night came rushing back to her. The voice at 3 a.m., the anger she felt, then somehow falling back to sleep only to have this dream. Daniel was the one she was supposed to tell. But, what would she tell him? She was sure he or anyone else would think she was a complete freak. She shook her head. She had just met this man. She was not about to get involved in his business.

Getting messages via dreams—and potentially from beyond—wasn't exactly foreign to Shelby. She had received a visit from her grandfather two months after he passed away last year. It was part of what convinced her that Laney may be on to something and not merely some brainwashed Portland hippie dippy. She had been in Kauai with her then-boyfriend and woke up to the sound of her grandfather speaking to her. She could smell him and feel his hand holding hers. Only, there wasn't anything there. She was so freaked out that she asked him to leave—she was too afraid.

He had asked her to be quiet, so he could tell her something, but she was too freaked out to hear what he had to say. Two nights later he tried again, visiting her in a dream with a message for her grandmother (who did not believe in the afterlife and would probably think Shelby was crazy). But, her grandfather had insisted that she deliver the message, even giving her some information about the electrical wiring in the house as proof. When Shelby called her grandmother the next morning, her grandma had been a bit cautious in her response, but did not write Shelby off the way she had imagined she would.

She had simply said, "You know, it's funny you mention the electricity here at the house (Shelby's grandfather had shown her a broken lamp in the living room with a frayed cord and indicated something could happen to cause a fire if it wasn't fixed)—we had an electrician out here yesterday because we were having problems."

Shelby had been ecstatic to hear this, because it meant she wasn't crazy (what a relief!), and her grandfather really had delivered a message to her. Her grandma continued, "Dreams are really funny, Shelby. I don't know where they come from, but they are certainly interesting."

This was her grandma's way of saying that Shelby's grandfather had also appeared in her dreams, but because her grandma didn't believe in the afterlife, she couldn't make sense of it.

So, even though Shelby had been overwhelmed by the visit from her grandfather, she felt good that she had delivered the message and that on some level her grandmother had been able to receive it. She had done the right thing.

But, giving Daniel a message seemed too far out of her comfort zone. Who was this woman anyway? And why was Shelby the only one who could give him this message? In any event, she had an out—she didn't have Daniel's contact information—so if that woman wanted the message to be delivered, she was going to have to make sure Daniel contacted Shelby.

Daniel was covered in sweat and completely flustered. He had torn apart his entire car, retraced his steps from his car to his studio and still he could not find Shelby's number. He had practically shredded his khaki pants in search for her number. It was nowhere to be found. He had considered calling the hotel to find out if someone had turned it in, but there were thousands of business cards being passed back and forth at the conference—no one would turn in a card at the front desk.

He was beside himself. Meeting Shelby had completely shifted his energy that day. Just looking into her eyes was like taking a walk on the beach, with a cool breeze blowing in whenever needed. Connecting with her had transformed him in some way and had completely altered the course of his big meeting with Kaley. Fully submerged in the bliss of having met Shelby, he was able to truly be himself, unattached to an outcome and passionate about his work. He had never had an experience like that before, and he definitely wanted more of it. In fact, if he hadn't met Shelby in person he would swear she was an angel.

Not being able to find her number was definitely making him think maybe Shelby had been an angel—only sent to him for that brief moment in time.

"If angels really exist, that is," Daniel mumbled under his breath.

Although he had been exploring the Law of Attraction in greater detail, even reading *The Law of Attraction* by Michael Losier, Daniel wasn't sure what he believed when it came to deeper spiritual topics like angels and the spirit world.

I've got to find her number. I'm starting to lose it speculating that she isn't even a real person!

The trouble was, Daniel didn't even have Shelby's last name. Daniel sat down on his couch, feeling defeated. He put his head in his hands; how could he have been so careless with her card? The excitement of meeting her and then going directly into his pitch meeting with Kaley had somehow caused him to lose the card. He had been careless and overzealous.

Daniel took a deep breath. He began a tapping technique called Cortices that one of his BodyTalk healing practitioners had given him. It helped balance the left and right sides of the brain, allowing him to calm down and think clearly. BodyTalk was a form of energy medicine that Daniel had used occasionally over the past few years whenever health issues came up in his life or whenever he felt stuck in some way. The healing always felt so good to him, but he often found himself unable to commit to a continued practice—it was as if some part of him enjoyed being stuck. He hadn't tapped in several months, and it felt good to do something other than freak out over the loss of Shelby's card. He took another deep breath and began tapping Cortices again.

Suddenly, he knew what he needed to do. He needed to meditate.

Daniel hadn't meditated in at least a year, as his primary focus for the past year had been writing his novel and becoming a successful writer. He didn't know how or when his meditation practice had stopped, but it had slipped away and, for some reason, in this moment he knew that's exactly what he needed to do. Several years prior, he had attended a Vipassana meditation retreat—and for 10 days he had not uttered a word, instead engaging in roughly 10 hours of meditation a day. After that he had maintained a solid meditation practice, sitting for 45 minutes to an hour almost daily.

Doing so had served him well. His life flowed with so much ease, making it possible for him to save up all the money he felt he needed before embarking on his journey of being a full-time writer. But, once the fear of not being successful gripped him, he had done nothing more than work tirelessly to force the writing and the subsequent success to come to him. This was yet another reason why he had been drawn to the Law of Attraction. His forcing and will-powering habits hadn't worked, although yesterday's events certainly seemed to indicate that things were beginning to shift.

Daniel arranged a blanket and pillows on the floor, and assumed his meditation position. He sat like that for 45 minutes. When he opened his eyes, he knew what he had to do next.

———

He revved the engine of his Subaru Outback, asking Daphne (he named his car this several years ago after dating a woman who followed the path of Hoʻoponopono, which believed everything was living and deserved respect. Daniel had to agree and loved the practice of naming everything—from his apartment to hotel rooms to his laptop—he found it created a sense of connection and warmth.) to get him to northwest Portland as quickly as possible. For some reason, he was feeling an intense urgency.

Winding through the streets of Portland, Daniel felt lighter. He was surprised how easily he was able to drop back into a meditative space. He didn't have to fight with his mind as much as he anticipated he would. Instead, he was able to reach that sweet place of surrender and bliss relatively easily. Even though going into the meditation he felt distressed about losing Shelby's phone number, he now felt that somehow it would all be okay.

And that's why he decided to follow the intense urge he had to go to his favorite coffee shop in northwest Portland. Despite not knowing exactly why he needed to be there.

That meditation must have really put me in the flow, Daniel thought as a parking spot right in front of CoffeeTime became available as he pulled up. His parallel parking skills were somehow much better than usual, as he skillfully guided Daphne into the spot. He jumped out of the car eager with anticipation; he couldn't wait to see what awaited him next.

The coffee shop was filled with the usual suspects—Portland hipsters and single girls with dogs, preferably pugs. Daniel loved CoffeeTime because it had open windows and doors that made for great people-watching and fresh air, especially during Portland's Indian summer months of September and October. He found it stimulated his creative juices, and often wrote poetry during his visits.

Today, he wasn't sure what he was going to do, but he figured he would let the Universe show him the way.

Daniel walked into the coffee shop and looked around. The smell of roasted coffee beans wafted in while the sounds of the espresso machine tinged with indie rock filled the air. Nothing seemed out of the ordinary, until he went up to the counter to order his usual decaf coffee. He casually turned to the right and saw a mass of blonde hair leaning over a piece of paper scribbling furiously.

It was Shelby.

Daniel stood frozen for several minutes.

"Excuse me, sir, would you like to order something?"

Daniel put his hand up and shook his head. He realized then that he was speechless. His mind was not able to process the series of events as quickly as they were occurring. It didn't make any sense. He had frequented this coffee shop at least weekly for a *year*. And never, never before had he seen that beautiful head of hair. Because Daniel's mind wasn't working at 100 percent, he walked right over to Shelby and stood there, still unable to speak.

Slowly, her frantic writing simmered as she looked up to see who was standing before her. When she got to Daniel's face, she smiled so big that she thought her cheeks might burst. Meanwhile, her mind tried to come up with all the ways and possibilities that he could have known she was at CoffeeTime (it didn't have much success, as the possibility was completely illogical). Then, her mind jumped in to remind her of the woman's voice, the dream and the message she was supposed to give Daniel. Because all of this was happening, she couldn't speak, there was too much to process.

So, they stood there looking at one another like that for what seemed like hours, but in truth was only a couple of minutes.

"Shelby. I am so glad to see you," Daniel finally sputtered.

"Daniel, I'm so glad to see you. How did you know I was here?"

"I didn't! That's what is so crazy. Can I sit down?"

"Oh, yes, of course! I'm sorry. Go ahead," Shelby scooted over so Daniel could join her in the booth. She turned to face him. "So, what got you here?"

"Well, I meditated for like the first time in forever, because I was freaking out that I had lost your number. I couldn't find it anywhere. I mean, I tore my entire car apart. I almost ripped those khaki pants I was wearing apart too. But, you know, I held back—they were really good khaki pants."

Shelby sat nodding and smiling, her mind attempting to understand the words he was saying. A meditation led him to the coffee shop she was at. Not finding her card had led him to meditate. She had been told to tell him to meditate. Shelby's inner dialogue screamed at her to say to him: SOME WOMAN CAME TO ME IN MY SLEEP LAST NIGHT AND TOLD ME TO TELL YOU TO MEDITATE AND THAT YOU NEEDED TO OPEN YOUR HEART. Instead, she said:

"They *were* really great khakis. I'm so grateful you didn't kill them over my number. But you lost my card?? How??"

It just seemed like a more sane response than what was screaming through her. And if Daniel noticed that there was more happening within her, he didn't show it. Probably because what he really wanted to say to Shelby was: I'M GOING TO GET A BOOK DEAL BECAUSE OF YOU AND I REALLY WANT TO SPEND MORE TIME WITH YOU AS SOON AS POSSIBLE. AND GOD, YOU LOOK GORGEOUS. But, instead he said:

"I have no clue how I managed to lose your card—it's so bizarre. But I meditated for 45 minutes and when I came out of it, I felt peaceful and like everything was going to be okay. And then I had this super strong urge to come here and I had no idea why, but knew that something was at play, so I followed it. And now look. You're here and I'm here. It's freakin' magic."

Shelby was totally stunned. It *was* magic. What were the odds? And did she even dare tell him about her dream last night?

"Wow, Daniel. That is magical. I'm sorry I'm not saying more. I literally feel speechless."

"I know, me too. And since we're here, can I buy you a cup of coffee or tea or a pastry—or do you want to go for a walk?"

"Actually, you know what?" Shelby said, grinning. "I'm up for all of the above."

3

The coffee turned into a walk and the walk turned into lunch. Daniel found himself having the best non-date date of his life.

By the time their lunch of grilled cheese sandwiches and tomato soup came around at The Huckleberry Pub on Northwest Kearney, Shelby decided she had to tell Daniel about her dream. Just looking at him made energy move in her body that she had never felt before—and he didn't even have to say anything. Throughout the day, she would look over at him and feel joy, simply from his presence. When he talked about his writing in such a passionate way, staring directly into her eyes, she melted. She wanted to tell him everything, about everything. She didn't care how crazy it sounded.

Daniel must have noticed her thoughts drifting as he paused, took a sip of his soup and asked, "Am I coming on too strong? Is this too intense?"

She found his slight bit of insecurity endearing. And she totally understood it. There had been many times in her life where she felt like she was too intense in relationships. No one could match her passion—not until now anyway. Daniel seemed to share that same trait with her and it gave her a tremendous amount of comfort.

"No! Not at all. In fact, I was admiring you as you spoke."

Daniel smiled, shaking his head. "You are something else Shelby. I don't know what is happening between us, but it is pretty incredible. I feel so grateful."

"I feel the same way Daniel. Very grateful. And you know, there is something I want to share with you that is also pretty incredible. It might sound kind of crazy, especially since we just met, but the timing of it all has me really curious. You up for it?"

Daniel's hazel eyes grew wide with anticipation. He looked like a cross between intrigued and freaked out. Shelby saw and felt his reaction immediately. She reached out and put her hand on his arm.

"Don't worry, I'm not about to reveal some deep, dark secret—not yet anyway. I had a very vivid dream last night and I'm wondering if you might be able to help me figure it out."

Shelby went on to share the details with Daniel, every last one, even the woman saying that Shelby was the one that could help him. Daniel watched Shelby carefully as she spoke. This made her slightly nervous, but she continued on, hoping that some part of him understood the message.

"So…I'm really curious who this woman might be and why she is telling me to connect with you. The fact that you meditated this very morning for the first time in a long time tells me that something magical is going on here, as that was part of her message to you. Do you have any thoughts about this?"

Shelby noticed that Daniels eyes were filling with tears.

"My mom died when I was 27," he blurted out. "Breast cancer. And when she was sick, I took it seriously, but not seriously enough. I didn't do enough to help her. Since she passed, I've been discovering all sorts of healing modalities that can help folks heal cancer and it kills me that I didn't do that work while she was still here—maybe some of it would have saved her life."

Shelby squeezed Daniel's arm and nodded. Goosebumps ran up her arms and legs. She knew it had to be his mother that was communicating with her.

"I loved her so much and I didn't show her enough. Ever since she passed, it's been so difficult for me to open myself up. I've spent so much time berating myself for not being a better son. I can't help but think that the woman and little boy you saw was me and my mom. I don't know why she's reaching out to you, though. I've never even had one dream with her in it in the past 11 years since she's been gone."

"I don't know either Daniel, but there is clearly a message that she is trying to send you. Are you open to regular meditation to see how that might shift things for you?"

"Yes, definitely. It's so wild that I haven't meditated in so long and then felt the inspiration to do so and it brought me to you."

Daniel looked lovingly into Shelby's eyes.

"I didn't know what I was going to do if I couldn't find your number. But, I didn't need to. The Universe—and apparently my mom—was leading me to you the whole time."

This time Daniel took Shelby's hand, gently moving it up to his mouth and kissing it, never once taking his eyes off of her.

Shelby could barely restrain herself, she wanted to reach across the table—allowing grilled cheese and tomato soup to land where it may—and kiss Daniel passionately. The electricity passing between them was powerful. Suddenly Shelby felt a soft breeze blow around her. She looked around but didn't see any windows open in the restaurant, and it was one of those Indian summer days with no clouds and no wind.

"You felt that too?"

Daniel was looking at her rather intently.

"You mean the breeze?"

"Yep. Where could that have come from?"

"I have no idea," Shelby said, continuing to look around as though a gust of wind through an open window or fan might suddenly appear to explain everything.

Goosebumps rose along her arms and legs again. She lifted her arm to show Daniel. "Something is going on."

"I'm feeling a chill all around me right now," Daniel said, sounding a bit concerned.

Shelby was curious, but not afraid. She wondered if his mom was around them now.

Tell him.

The hairs on her arms and the back of her neck rose.

Tell him, Shelby.

Shelby had no idea what more she needed to tell him. And she was still having trouble making sense of the fact that Daniel's deceased mother was communicating with her.

Tell him I'm proud of him. Tell him, Shelby.

Something must have changed in her face during this because Daniel became concerned, holding her hand tighter.

"Shelby, what's going on? Your eyes just drifted off, you looked like you went somewhere else far away."

He's definitely going to think I'm insane if I tell him this, Shelby thought. I'll tell him later, like I did with the dream, she decided.

"Oh nothing, just tripping out about the dream, the breeze, the chills and everything. I've never really experienced anything like this before."

Daniel stood up.

"I know! Me either. But honestly, I'm so glad you're here. I would be spooked if I was left to experience this on my own with no one to share the play-by-play with. Do you want to get out of here?"

Tell him Shelby, he needs to know this.

Shelby flipped her hair hoping his mom would get the hint that it wasn't going to happen right now.

"Sure! Where to next?"

Shelby stood up and turned to grab her purse. She felt a bit off kilter and stumbled forward. She felt Daniel as he put his hands on her waist.

"You okay?" he said, pulling her in closer to him.

Shelby turned around to face him.

"Well, I'm much better now."

Daniel looked down at her (she was 5'4 to his 5'11) and smiled.

"You are incredibly beautiful, you know that, don't you?"

She wanted him to kiss her so badly she could barely breathe.

Tell him Shelby. He has to hear this and it has to come from you.

His mother was beginning to get on her nerves. Couldn't she see they were getting intimate right now? Shelby wrapped her arms around Daniel more closely and hugged him tightly. He responded, his arms extending over her hips, the side of his face pressed into hers. He smelled like vanilla with spices mixed in. She felt Daniel's face tilt towards her and she slowly leaned her head back. Their noses were touching and he smiled softly.

"May I kiss you, Shelby?"

"Right here in this restaurant?"

"Right here, right now."

Shelby pushed her body closer in to Daniel's, whispering, "Yes."

His lips touched hers lightly at first and then began pressing into her more firmly. He pushed his body into hers and the two of them were standing so close not even a breeze could have moved between them. Shelby responded with a soft moan. He tasted like vanilla and mint and…and…she wasn't sure, but whatever it was, it was delicious. His tongue flicked inside her mouth and Shelby felt her panties get wet. She wanted him right there, right now. His erection pushed into her more firmly as their lips stayed intertwined. She could have stood there like that (with maybe a few less clothes on) forever.

Except that damn voice kept coming in.

Shelby, tell him I'm proud of him. Do it now.

Shelby pulled back, looked into Daniel's eyes and said, "Thank you." Then she wrapped her arms around him more tightly.

Shelby. If you don't tell him now—

"Okay! Fine! Jesus Christ, just leave me alone."

Daniel pulled back with a start.

"What? What did you say?"

Shelby was now 50 different shades of red.

"I'm so sorry Daniel—I didn't mean to say that to you. It's, well, there's more than the dream happening right now. I'm getting some kind of message for you."

Just then the waitress came by. "You two all finished?"

Daniel didn't take his eyes off Shelby, "We're going to need a few more minutes here."

The waitress must have felt the intensity in their exchange, as she quickly turned and walked away.

"You're getting messages for me? From who? My mom?"

"I know. This is crazy. But yes, I think so."

"Okay, yeah, this is nearing crazy-town. What did she say?"

They were standing face to face, no longer touching, but still close enough to kiss. Shelby cursed his mother's poor timing; his lips seemed to be calling her name. Nevermind that now though, she had to focus on delivering the message.

"Well, okay. She is very emphatically instructing me and she is quite demanding—but you may already know that."

She looked up, Daniel wasn't smiling. Shit, Shelby thought. Humor may not coincide with delivering messages from the other side very well.

"She says—um—she says that she's— "

"Please just say it. I'm dying over here."

"She says she's proud of you. And it's important that you know that."

Daniel's eyes once again filled with tears, he looked down and put both hands to his face. It seemed like the room was spinning.

"Do you want to sit down? I'm sorry Daniel, I don't know what's going on any more than you do."

Daniel nodded and sat back in the chair. His head was spinning now, as flashes of his childhood, adolescence, his twenties and now his thirties flashed before him. He had to leave, he had to get out of there.

"I have to go Shelby. I have to go." Daniel said as he looked up. "I appreciate you giving me this message and sharing with me about the dream, but I've been blocking feeling this for a long time and I can't process this right now and in front of you. I have to go. We'll talk later."

Shelby's heart sank. She had scared him. She hadn't meant to and she was only following the message coming in, but it was too late. She nodded and pulled out her *Hello Portland* business card.

"So, I'll try again. Here's my card."

Daniel took it and managed to give her a feeble smile.

"I won't lose it this time," He opened up his wallet and placed it inside.

4

And inside his wallet is where Shelby's card stayed.

Daniel went home that afternoon reeling. How could his mother be proud of him? He hadn't done anything he set out to. He wasn't living the life she would have wanted for him. She wanted him to get married, have a family, be responsible and work a normal job like everyone else.

"Daniel, honey, life is much easier than you make it out to be. And it starts with love. When you love others, the rest unfolds as it's meant to. You can't force becoming a great novelist like Steinbeck. You only need to find love and the rest will come."

She used to tell him that over and over again.

Well, he was 38 now and he wasn't doing any of that. And to make matters worse, he had let her down by not being a better son during her illness. He didn't want to believe she could really be sick, so sick that she might die. And she had put up a good face and told him it was fine to take the trip to Europe. He would never forget that day.

She was home, with her sisters and brothers there taking care of her. Daniel's dad bounced in and out of their lives, but never stayed around too long. Daniel went on weekend visits with him up until age 11, but after that quit seeing him altogether. He never felt comfortable with him. His dad loved to drink and point out where others were wrong. If Daniel was around when his father was drinking, all he heard was how he would never amount to anything.

So when Daniel's mom got sick with cancer at age 56, it was her family that came together and rallied around her, supporting her through it. He wished he had been a more integral part of that process. He let himself fade into the background as his aunts and uncles took care of his mom.

The morning he told her about the opportunity to take a trip to Europe with a few friends, she was pale and a bit out of breath, but in good spirits. She was sitting on the patio, dressed in a white bathrobe, sipping peppermint tea. It felt like only yesterday that they had the conversation.

"What do you want to talk to me about, Daniel?" she had said, her blue eyes still revealing a faint light.

"Mom, I know you haven't been feeling well (Daniel realizes now this was pretty much the understatement of the year, as she had been sick for six months at this point), but I have an opportunity to go to London with some friends in a few weeks and I wanted to see how you felt about that."

She had smiled at the mention of London, a place she had visited once, long ago, when she was in her early twenties. It was a time of great adventure and love. She had fallen in lust with a pub owner-slash-motorcycle rider that summer. Tattooed and tan, they had spent weeks rolling around in bed together followed by going out visiting all the sights in London. She giggled softly to herself.

"Mom??"

"Oh, sorry love. I was reminiscing about the last time I was in London. It is such a fun place to visit, especially when you're young." She had winked at him then.

Her eyes drifted far off into the distance and Daniel could feel that she was revisiting London yet again, no longer sitting there with him.

He touched her hand.

"Are you okay mom?"

"Oh yes, I'm fine—minus the breast cancer, of course." She smiled feebly, somewhat proud of her ability to make light of a situation that had seemed so dark to everyone else. She patted his hand and said, "You go and do whatever you need to and I'll be right here when you get back. Don't you worry."

Daniel leaned in and kissed her cheek.

"Thanks mom. I love you."

"I love you too, dear. Now go get your aunt Ali and tell her I am in need of some sliced fruit and juice. All that London reminiscing has made me hungry."

Daniel had smiled then thinking to himself that she would be fine and one day things would go back to normal, with her taking painting classes, traveling to Paris and anywhere else she wanted to go.

But that didn't happen. Instead, the day Daniel was set to fly back from his trip, his Aunt Ali called him with the news.

"She's gone Daniel," she had said in between sobs.

Daniel stood in the airport, stunned, unable to move. People moved all around him, but he couldn't even see them. All he could see was that far off look in her eyes and that white gown. A cold breeze washed over him and he crumpled to the floor crying.

From that moment forward, Daniel's heart closed. He could never allow himself to love anyone again, especially another woman who could also leave him.

The pain of allowing himself to feel all of the various emotions around his mother's death was too much for Daniel to handle. He had allowed himself that one day in the airport. After that, he had not let himself cry over her passing. Meeting Shelby had shifted something within him, but his conditioned way of behaving and his ego were stronger. So, he did what he always did, and threw himself back into his work. He began making edits to his novel and checking his email in hopes of hearing from Kaley Hamilton with good news.

Daniel didn't have to wait long. Two weeks after he last saw Shelby, he received the following email from Kaley Hamilton:

Dear Daniel,

It was such a pleasure meeting you a few weeks ago at the Willamette Writers Conference. Your confidence and talent definitely got my attention.

I have finished reading your manuscript and feel like we might have something very valuable to work with. I am headed off to a writing retreat in Maui, Hawaii, and would love to have you join me, so we can go over the manuscript, make some adjustments and begin pitching it to publishers.

There were be a host of publishers at this intimate and exclusive retreat, and I feel it's the perfect opportunity to share your writing with some big players in the publishing game. It's also a wonderful opportunity for us to further develop our partnership!

The details for the retreat location, dates, and costs are all included at the end of this email. Please let me know at once if you can be there. I know it's last-minute, but careers like John Steinbeck's have an expiration date. The sooner we move forward the better!

Warmly,

Kaley

Daniel could hardly believe his eyes. Maui? Kaley Hamilton? Publishers? A career like Steinbeck's? It was as if the Universe was delivering to him exactly what he had always wanted, but in a way he had never imagined.

He shook his head and read it again.

No, as it turns out, he wasn't dreaming. The costs were steep, but Daniel still had some money tucked away with over $10,000 that he could use to fund the trip. It was the opportunity of a lifetime and he could not turn it down.

"So, does your food cart adhere to the state health code for restaurants?" Shelby asked the owner of Sweet Thai, yet another Thai food cart located in Portland's downtown. She was working on a piece about the food cart phenomenon for *Hello Portland* and couldn't help but focus in on the health concerns. Not all of the carts seemed that up to code.

As she was listening to the man, her digi-recorder held up to capture his response, something out of the corner of her eye caught her attention. She could have sworn it was Daniel. He was practically speed walking into the Portland Luggage store, although she wasn't 100 percent sure it was him.

"Okay, yes, that's great, thanks so much. I just remembered that I have to go to the Portland Luggage store. Right now. Thanks for your time," Shelby interrupted the food cart owner (who in hindsight she felt badly for, with her rushing off the way she did), quickly making her way over to where she had seen Daniel. There were about 50 Thai food carts in Portland, she could find another cart owner to interview at a time when Daniel wasn't in the area—she was sure of it.

It had been two and a half weeks and she hadn't heard a thing from Daniel since their first, and so far only, date. She knew giving him the message from his mother had overwhelmed him, but she couldn't believe he wouldn't at least follow up with an email or something. Their connection had been so strong that it simply didn't make any sense to Shelby that he would outright ignore it.

Seeing him on the street meant something and she would be damned if she let him walk on by. Shelby picked up the pace as she came upon the store, silently cursing the 2-inch red heels she had let Kathryn talk her into buying. Although, they were absolutely perfect for seeing Daniel again, just not for race-walking down sidewalks.

Shelby stealthily slid into the Portland Luggage store, on full alert. She had no idea what she was going to say to Daniel or how she was going to approach the fact that he had blown her off, but she was going to do it. She didn't have connections like that very often with men, and she would completely regret it if she didn't take some type of action.

It was, however, beyond her to know exactly what action she should take. Hiding behind a large display of oversized suitcases, Shelby began texting Kathryn, giving her the 4-1-1 on the situation. She prayed that as a fellow writer, Kathryn would be in her home office, in front of the computer with her cellphone nearby. Fortunately, she was and the reply came in quickly, although it wasn't exactly what Shelby had hoped she would say:

Stop hiding! Center urself in ur heart rt now, see green light all around ur heart and then go up to him. Let ur intuition guide u. It will know what 2 say.

Really? She would miraculously know what to say? That honestly was not much of a plan. She gave Kathryn the middle finger (in her mind, of course) and stepped out from behind the suitcases. Daniel was exactly kitty-corner from her, looking at some backpack, laptop combo bag. Shelby didn't know what else to do, so she went with Kathryn's advice. She moved her focus from her mind, which was in hyper-chatter mode, and into her heart. She visualized a green ball of light emanating from her chest. At that exact moment, Daniel spun around as though a laser beam had hit him from behind.

His mouth dropped open.

Shelby smiled.

Kathryn had known what she was talking about after all.

———

It took Daniel a few moments to collect himself. He had been so deep in thought about what bag would give him the most room and would be the easiest to trek to Maui with, that he was completely startled when he felt a rush of heat and energy surround him from behind and move into his heart. He spun around, unsure of what he might see, and even more stunned to see Shelby standing there smiling back at him.

Was the heat and rush of energy from her? He felt a bit dizzy. He began to remember that she had this effect on him. As all of this was running through his now frazzled mind, she walked over to him. He couldn't help but reflect on how unbelievably beautiful she was. Her blonde hair was piled on top of her head in a messy yet perfectly styled manner, her bangs dropping slightly into her gorgeous blue eyes. She was wearing a black pencil skirt with a black top, but what really got his attention were her bright red heels. She looked gorgeous.

He opened his mouth to say something, but nothing came out.

"Looks as though you're as stunned as I am," Shelby said, looking up at him rather coyly.

"You look beautiful," was all he could get out.

Her face softened.

"Thank you, that's so sweet." The line in her brow creased. "Were you beginning to forget what I looked like?"

He could sense her displeasure in his obvious lack of communication in the past two-and-a-half weeks. At the moment, he couldn't remember why he hadn't called her back or what was delaying him from not spending every day with her. He shook his head.

"Shelby. I'm sorry. It's far more complicated than that, I—"

"Well then, tell me about it. Disappearing on me only to have the Universe find random ways to reconnect us might become a little exhausting over time."

She didn't want to sound irritated, but she was. She wanted to scream at him! *How can you have such a wonderful, loving connection with someone—like a once in a lifetime connection—and not call them? Not even text them?!*

Instead, she looked up at him and sighed with disdain.

Daniel smiled sweetly at her. She didn't want it to work, but it did, and she softened yet again. Somewhere she could hear Kathryn in the distance yelling at her "green light!"

"Listen, you're right," Daniel said. "Avoiding each other only means the Universe has to work harder. I totally agree. I'm surprised, but I agree. And honestly, since we met, so much has happened, I really want to tell you all about it."

"And I would love to hear it. But first, why are you surprised?"

"Well, uh, I've never had such obvious interference by the Universe to make sure I connected with someone. It's a bit eerie."

"Or awesome," Shelby laughed.

"Or awesome, you're right."

"So, what are you doing at the luggage store on a random Wednesday anyway?"

Daniel still had the molten red backpack laptop, carry-all in his hand. He held it down to her heels.

"I was trying to find something for you that would match those killer heels."

They both laughed.

"I wish you would. I literally can only wear black with them," Shelby responded.

"In all seriousness, I got this incredible opportunity to go to Maui and meet with this agent. She wants to go over my manuscript and share it with some publishers that are going to be there for this small retreat."

"Wow! Congratulations! That seems like a long way to go to review your manuscript, but it's Maui—so who cares, right?"

"I know, I had the same thought. But this could be my big break, so I'm going for it."

"God, that's really great Daniel. When do you leave?"

"I leave next Friday morning. But honestly, I have to thank you Shelby. Our connection at the writer's conference allowed me to breeze through the meeting with Kaley Hamilton and then land this opportunity."

Shelby groaned inside. Kaley Hamilton? She was notorious for bedding her authors. And while she did have an eye for a good story, her true focus always seemed to be on sleeping with her authors first. Did Daniel have any idea that she was most likely on the hunt for him? Shelby knew one thing, she wasn't going to be the one to break the news to him. The last time she shared an intuition with him, he avoided her for over two weeks.

Shelby looked into Daniel's eyes to give her best fake, blasé response. Just as she was about to open her mouth, she felt a wave of heat pass through her body and into her pelvis. It caught her so off guard that she wobbled a little. Daniel reached out to steady her, placing both of his strong hands on her upper arms.

"Shelby, are you okay? You looked like you were going to say something, but then it seemed like you might fall over."

Shelby began fanning her face. First heart light energy and then this, she had no idea what was going on.

"Oh, I'm fine, I'm fine." She feigned.

Daniel took her by the hand, "C'mon, let's get you outside into some fresh air."

Shelby was pleasantly surprised by his firm handle on the situation, and she happily followed.

He led her to a bench outside the store. He sat down with her and then turned to face her. This time both of his hands were on hers.

"Okay, Shelby, you have to know something. I'm crazy attracted to you, but I'm also crazy terrified of you. When I turned around in the store back there, I had felt some wild warmth and almost like a hot poker in my upper back. Then, just now, when you went to say something and almost fainted, I felt this wave of warmth spread through my whole body—so intensely I felt like *I* might fall over. I don't know what is going on with our connection, but it's powerful. The messages you got from my mom completely spun me out. I've been spending the past 11 years feeling like a failure as her son and I don't know what to make of the information you're receiving from her. Not to mention, I'm on my way to Maui, for what will hopefully be a game-changer for my life and my career."

Shelby looked back at him in a state of shock. She was grateful he was being so honest with her, but she also didn't know how to respond. She looked down at her hands, the hands he was holding. She loved the look of them, their fingers entwined, his strong hands holding on to hers so firmly yet gently. She wished she had a camera so she could take a photograph of their hands. It seemed like they belonged together.

"Daniel, thank you for being so honest with me. And I'm sorry that our connection is also terrifying to you. I feel so drawn to you and I've been confused as to why it seems to send you in the other direction. What I do know is that we don't have to make sense of it right now. Go on your trip and if when you get back, you feel less crazy-terrified and more crazy-attracted, then let's go from there."

Tears welled up in Shelby's eyes as she said this. She didn't know if she would ever see him again after this trip. Who wouldn't fall in love with Maui and a lucrative writing career? Her heart chakra was pulsating so strongly, she was having trouble catching her breath.

"Well, I don't leave for another week. Maybe we could spend a bit more time together until then," Daniel heard himself say. He didn't know why, but that sense of urgency was back. He had to spend more time with this girl.

And Shelby, despite wanting to play it cool until he was back from Maui and the greedy arms of Kaley Hamilton, eagerly shook her head yes.

5

It was while picnicking over Pinot Gris, goat cheese, rice crackers, olives and salami in the Rose Gardens that Daniel realized that part of him was falling in love with Shelby. Part of him was also already in Maui having the best career of his life. But, the part that was sitting in front of this gorgeous girl, just wanted more time with her—as much time as he could have.

They were sharing childhood stories over wine, while enjoying the spectacular views of the city. Shelby felt more at ease than she ever had with a man and did everything she could to brush thoughts of Kaley Hamilton and Maui out of her mind. Two more days were left; she didn't have to think about it yet.

"So, what's your favorite memory from childhood?" Shelby asked.

"Oh, that's easy—scrambled eggs."

"Scrambled eggs? I'm going to need more details on this."

"Well, every Sunday morning my mom would get up early and make us all a huge breakfast. It was one of our favorite things to look forward to on the weekends. We didn't have a lot of money growing up, so it was the little things that mattered. Mom would make bacon, scrambled eggs with cheese, pancakes, biscuits—the works. We literally only had to eat one meal on Sundays. But her scrambled eggs were absolutely the best. She had this secret—she would fry up the bacon first in the skillet and then add the bacon grease to the eggs."

Shelby crinkled her nose.

"And that was good?"

"Yep, absolutely the best," Daniel said, as he took a sip of wine looking out over the Rose Gardens. They were sitting in the amphitheater, giving them an outstanding view of the gardens and some of the city.

Daniel put his arm around Shelby and sighed. Life was very good. The past three days with Shelby had flown by. They had gone on a hike in Forest Park, went to Working Class acupuncture for a community session and had enjoyed Portland's well-known food cart scene on several occasions (giving Shelby the chance to finish up the piece she had been working on when she saw Daniel at the Portland Luggage store). Each day they did something different, and each day the connection felt stronger. Their kiss after lunch weeks ago had now progressed into some of the most passionate make-out sessions of his life. It took everything in his power to not rip all of Shelby's clothes off.

Shelby leaned over and kissed his neck. Small, light kisses, trickling up to his ear. And this is when Daniel got into trouble. She kissed around his ear, lightly licking and biting around the edges. Daniel held her more tightly, feeling his erection growing. Shelby must have felt it too, as she placed her hand discreetly on his hardness, rubbing him gently.

"Shelby, you're driving me crazy," Daniel whispered.

"That's the point," she whispered back.

He chuckled. "Well, you certainly know what you're doing."

Shelby smiled, moving her hand over to his thigh as another couple walked through the amphitheater.

"What, you're not an exhibitionist?" Daniel inquired.

"Not quite yet. Although, I suppose I could be convinced," she said as she winked.

"Damn people in the Rose Garden."

"I know, didn't they get the memo that it was all ours?" Shelby joked.

"Well, maybe it's a sign to head out. We've pretty much devoured this entire log of goat cheese," Daniel looked down at the few nibbles of goat cheese, crackers, and grapes that were left.

They stood up and began wrapping up their food and wine. Daniel went to get his keys.

"Oh shit. Do you have the keys, babe?"

Daniel was surprised to hear those words come out of his mouth. He hadn't called a woman babe in—well, never.

"Uh, no. Don't you?"

"I can't find them. Damn."

They both stared at each other. They had spent some time walking through the park, admiring the flowers. Daniel had even picked Shelby up and carried her through one section of roses. He wondered if he had dropped them then.

"I need to retrace my steps to see if I can find them. You stay here and look around and see if they fell out of my pocket and into the grass somewhere. I'll be right back."

Daniel looked stressed and Shelby wasn't sure what she could do. The last time she saw him with the keys was when they had gotten out of the car and were walking into the Rose Garden. As she walked around where they had been sitting looking for his keys, Shelby noticed that darkness was descending upon them and the park was mostly empty.

"Shit, shit, shit. Not a great way to end a perfectly romantic evening," she muttered under her breath.

Shelby had been contemplating whether to sleep with Daniel before he left for Maui. Their connection was so intense that it had been difficult to control herself. Just *thinking* about the possibility of having Daniel inside of her made her wet. Besides, they had really only spent the past week together—could she really sleep with him so soon? She also had to contend with her distrust of Kaley Hamilton. What if Kaley seduced Daniel and things fell apart? She wasn't sure she could risk it.

Focus, Shelby, focus. She had to remind herself.

She crouched down on the grass in front of where they had been sitting, feeling with her hands and straining her eyes to see if the keys were hiding somewhere in the grass. It was a few inches longer than usual, she thought, making it more difficult to see. She leaned down further, as something sparkly caught her eye.

It was then that she felt a breeze flow past her. She thought it odd, as it had been a quiet, still night, but she dismissed the thought and went to pick up the silver item in the grass. Unfortunately, it was only a bottle wrapper and not Daniel's keys. She felt the breeze again, only this time, it felt like it was coming from the opposite direction. This time Shelby felt goosebumps rise up and down her arms.

Shelby.

She heard a soft woman's voice say her name. She looked up quickly, hitting her head on the cement edged benches that were built into the amphitheater. Grabbing her head, Shelby jumped up.

"Is someone there?" She hadn't seen anyone in the garden since Daniel left.

Shelby. It's me. Over here, to your right.

The goosebumps covered Shelby's arms and up her neck. She looked to her right and saw a wispy outline of what appeared to be a woman.

"Oh. My. God." Shelby had never seen a ghost like this before and felt a strong impulse to run, screaming Daniel's name. Instead she cupped her hands to her mouth.

Don't be afraid, my dear. The woman said as her wispy outline swayed softly. *I'm here to help you. I'm here to help Daniel too.*

"Are, are, oh my god, are you Daniel's mother? The one who has been talking to me in my head??"

The wispy woman chuckled gently. *Well, I'm not actually in your head when that happens. Your auditory senses are merely translating my vibration into words in your mind. I'm usually standing right next to you. But technicalities, right?*

Shelby was officially freaked out. Receiving messages from

and connecting with the other side was fine as long as she didn't have to see anything. This was too much.

I understand this is unusual dear, but tonight the lighting and situation were too perfect to pass up. It's easier to appear when it's in a setting you aren't normally accustomed to. But, let's not waste time with all of the semantics—it takes a lot of energy for me to appear to you like this, so I want to make it quick. You need to go to Maui with Daniel, dear. He needs you there.

Shelby laughed. This woman was going to a lot of trouble to give her such preposterous messages.

"Don't you need to be saving a life or keeping our government or economy from imploding or something? Is this really what we do after we die, try to hook up our loved ones?"

Shelby didn't mean to be disrespectful, but this was becoming too much. She was having a hard enough time processing her feelings for Daniel, especially with him leaving so soon. Having to deal with a dead mother who wanted them together seemed a bit to over the top to her. It was also making her seriously question her own sanity.

Oh, Shelby. The woman sighed, her wispy figure swaying slightly. *There is so much you don't know about the non-physical when you are in your physical body. We have the advantage of knowing so much more about the big picture of what's happening in the world. It's a vantage point that is quite challenging to hold objectively when in the body. I can assure you that this is about far more than Daniel and you hooking up, as you say. To keep things simple, my assignment is not to save the government or your silly economic system—don't even get me started on all of that nonsense. What I can tell you now is, I am here to save a life, and part of that includes you going with Daniel to Maui.*

"I would love to go with Daniel to Maui, but there's one little problem. He hasn't invited me. And we've only been technically spending time together for a week. Oh, and perhaps you've noticed that he was invited there by Kaley Hamilton, an agent who is almost more well known for seducing her authors than she is for her professional work."

Ah, yes, length of time and seduction. I forgot how much humans worry about time and the rightness of things. So busy worrying and judging, you miss out on all of the fun.

The woman started fading further away, it looked like she was drifting off. Shelby felt relieved and frightened at the same time. How was she supposed to bridge this subject with Daniel? He hadn't exactly enjoyed her last messages from his mother. And whose life needed to be saved anyway? Daniel's? Kaley Hamilton's? Hers?

"Wait! Daniel totally shuts down when I give him messages from you. How do I tell him this without scaring him half to death?"

The wispy figure disappeared. All Shelby heard was a faint, *Leave. That. To. Me.*

And then she was gone. Shelby looked around the amphitheater. It was completely empty, not a soul was in sight. She looked where the woman had been floating and now there was simply a small, motionless, bush. The breeze was completely gone. Shelby sat down on one of the benches, dumbfounded. She didn't know what to do. She wanted to tell Daniel, but she needed to think things through before doing that. Maybe Kathryn could help her with this dilemma. At least she wouldn't freak out on her. Kathryn loved stuff like this. She leaned over, placing her hands on her temples, rubbing them softly. Where was Daniel anyway?

―――

Daniel kicked the gravel and cursed. He had been so immersed in Shelby that he hadn't thought to pay attention to something important like his keys. What was wrong with him? In two days, he would be getting on a plane to Maui to meet with the highly successful Kaley Hamilton, as well as potential publishers—why wasn't he more focused or nervous or something? When he was around Shelby, he felt peaceful and calm, his mind unencumbered by details and deadlines and…well, apparently his keys as well.

He had retraced his steps, but to no avail. He even checked the spot where he had decided to impulsively scoop Shelby up into his arms and twirl her around the gardens. He was sure he would have heard them fall out of his sweatshirt, but maybe not. She was so beautiful and so…easy to be with. She felt like his best friend already and they barely knew one another.

Daniel decided he would have to head back to where Shelby was and see about calling AAA or someone to help. Perhaps if they could get back to her car, she could take him to his place where his spare car keys were. But damn, that would require having his house key, which of course, was on his car key set. A rustling in the rose bush over on his right interrupted his strategic planning process. It was filled with beautiful purple roses, but it was also now swaying unnaturally. He wondered if a possum or raccoon had gotten stuck in some of the brush inside of it.

Invite Shelby to go to Maui with you.

The thought randomly popped into his mind. Daniel stopped walking and looked around. Where had that come from? It wasn't like a voice from someone else, but it also wasn't his own thought. Asking Shelby to go on what was essentially a business trip and quite possibly the big break of his life was out of the question. He had no idea what to expect and he certainly couldn't ask her to come along when he himself didn't know what was going to take place. Besides, he wanted to appear as though he were a professional to Kaley Hamilton, not some guy who brings a girl he's only known one week to Maui for the signing of his book deal (in Daniel's imagination, the entire deal would happen on this trip—he was visualizing his intended outcome daily).

Daniel mentally sorted through the pros and cons of the thought. Shelby was a really spectacular girl. Going anywhere with her had been so much fun, he couldn't imagine that Maui would be any different.

But still, the trip was only two days away. Impossible. She wouldn't be able to get the time off work or even have the money for a trip like that.

You have enough money to pay for her. And she hates her job anyway.

He tossed these "thoughts" aside and picked up his stride to make it back to where Shelby was. It was dark now and he realized he had left her alone for quite some time—that was the opposite of being a gentleman, lost keys or not.

Take Shelby to Hawaii Daniel.

Again! Where was that thought coming from? Hadn't he decided that it was illogical to ask her at this point in the game with everything that was going on? And why were thoughts entering into his mind in the third person? He was stunned. Something unusual was definitely happening. He looked down at his arm, noticing goosebumps everywhere. Just then, he felt a slight breeze blow on the back of his neck.

He came up to where he and Shelby had been sitting to see Shelby crouched down, her head in her hands.

"Shelby?"

She didn't seem to hear him. A knot formed in his stomach.

"Shelby?" He walked closer.

He touched her shoulder and she jumped up, startled.

"Okay, yeah, well yes, bake those cookies for 20 minutes Kathryn and then yeah, they will be done. Oh, and thanks for AAA's number. Okay, love ya, yeah, bye!" Shelby said quickly as she wrapped up her call with Kathryn.

"So sorry about that Daniel. You startled me. I looked everywhere for the keys and when they didn't turn up, I thought I would call Kathryn to see if she or Scott had any good ideas about what we could do. They said try AAA if you had another car key at home and your landlord could let you into your place."

Daniel hugged her, tightly.

"Oh, I was so worried something was wrong. I had the weirdest walk—things were feeling kind of spooky. I felt terrible when I realized how long I left you out here alone. And then when I saw you crouched down like that…"

His voice trailed off, Shelby could hear emotion rising in his voice.

"I thought maybe something had happened to you..."

He squeezed her tighter, his hand holding the back of her hair, stroking it softly. Shelby instantly relaxed in his arms. His touch, the way he held her—it was as if they were a perfect fit.

Shelby leaned back, placing her hands on either side of Daniel's face.

"Well, I'm fine sweetie. Nothing to worry about at all. But thank you for caring so much."

Shelby couldn't figure out why she just called him sweetie. It had been a week for crying out loud. She admonished herself to slow down, and then smiled thinking back to what Daniel's mother had said about humans and timeframes.

"What's the smile about?"

"Oh, no—nothing. I was merely reflecting on the situation we're in, yet it all feels like it's totally fine standing here like this."

Shelby was grateful she had the ability to think on her feet.

Daniel smiled back at her, his arms snugly wrapped around her waist.

"You know what Shelby? You are absolutely right. I was thinking about that on my walk back actually, how being with you feels easy and…right…"

They looked into each other's eyes, smiling but not saying a word. Daniel had half a mind to lay Shelby down right there in the Rose Garden lawn and make love to her. If only he had his keys. Oh yes, his keys. How could he forget? Although looking into Shelby's eyes had a way of making him forget quite a bit.

Daniel leaned down and placed his lips tenderly on Shelby's. Their mouths intertwined softly, deliberately, as if each knew exactly what the other wanted and needed. He felt her tongue stroke his and immediately he was aroused. They stood there like that for several minutes, before the thought of the darkness, the closing of the park, and the keys entered their reality yet again.

They pulled back, looking at each other with longing and knowing. What was happening between them was far bigger than either of them could have imagined.

As they walked hand-in-hand back to the car, they looked for the keys one final time. On the way they created a plan: if they didn't find the keys by the time they got to the car, they would contact Rose Garden security, Daniel's landlord and Kathryn for a ride to his place.

Daniel noticed that he didn't feel as tense about the whole situation as he had initially. Being in Shelby's presence and talking through solutions with her made everything feel easier. When they got to the car, Daniel noticed something shiny and silver on the rooftop of Daphne, his green Subaru wagon.

"What the hell— "

He walked over to Daphne to find his keys sitting right on top of the roof. Daniel held them up before Shelby, bewildered.

Shelby, on the other hand, couldn't contain herself. She burst out laughing. She was laughing so hard she was leaning over gasping for air.

"What's so funny there, missy?"

"The keys," Shelby gasped in between laughs, "were on top of," she could barely get the words out, "the car!"

"Yes, I see that. And however do you think they got there?" Shelby's laughter was so hilarious that he was close to busting at the seams as well.

"Your mom." Shelby was doubled over. She couldn't believe it. The whole key incident had been orchestrated by his mother. She knew it.

"My mom?" Now Daniel wasn't laughing. And he was pretty sure Shelby was delusional. "My mom is dead Shelby." Suddenly he got very serious.

Shelby stopped laughing. Shit. Her and her big mouth.

"I know Daniel. But you know how people say that when our loved ones cross over they often come back to give us messages or play with us?" She was really hoping he would follow her lead on this one. She hadn't been able to finish her conversation with Kathryn, so she didn't have a full plan in place. Kathryn told her not to mention it until they could intuitively feel into the situation more and devise a better plan. But already Daniel was beginning to feel like her best friend and it was difficult to keep things from him.

"No. I don't know too much about that kind of thing. But if my mom did do this, she must have had some reason beyond just giving me shit."

Shelby breathed a sigh of relief, he wasn't going to lose it and shut down on her.

"Well, it was a thought. How do you think they ended up there?"

"I haven't the slightest idea," Daniel said. The mention of his mother made him think about the rustling in the rose bush, the eerie feeling in the air and how taking Shelby to Maui had popped into his mind—seemingly out of nowhere. Maybe Shelby was on to something. Maybe his mom *was* trying to get his attention. Although honestly, he thought, she was going to have to be a lot more direct if she wanted to get any sort of message through to him.

6

"Okay, so one more time Shelby," Kathryn said the next day as she stood in tree pose, sipping a steaming cup of green tea in her living room the following morning. "You saw her as a wispy outline of a woman and she told you that 1) it was taking her a lot of energy to present herself to you in that way—a topic we do need to explore at another time, and 2) that you needed to go to Maui with Daniel. And he leaves the day after tomorrow on this trip? And when do you see him next?"

"Yes, ma'am, that is it," Shelby replied. She knew it sounded outrageous, but at the same time wickedly interesting. She had never before in her life had such a mystical experience and she had absolutely zero idea how to handle it. "And I see him tonight, then tomorrow for lunch and after that it's all completely out of my hands."

She had brought Laney along as well, figuring the more intuitive beings she had helping her through this conundrum, the better. Laney was curled up on Kathryn's cream sofa, her dirty blonde locks swept up on top of her head, and two knitting needles in her hand. Laney had recently taken up knitting, promising that she would be making scarves for all four sisters for the upcoming holidays.

"I don't understand why Shelby is getting to have all of the cool non-physical experiences. I thought I was the woo-woo one in our family," Laney jokingly whined.

"Oh stop, you," Shelby faux-swatted at her. "I need real help here. Focus."

"Scott, you've got to come in here," Kathryn called into the other room. "Shelby communicated with a dead person last night." The sound of the words "dead person" brought Scott immediately into the living room, placing his hand on the small of Kathryn's back as she stood in tree pose, kissing her on the lips. "You are so beautiful. Isn't she beautiful?" Scott asked Shelby and Laney.

"The most beautiful." They giggled in unison. Laney rolled her eyes, pretending to be uninterested in Scott's love for Kathryn. The truth was, although Laney said she wasn't ready for a serious relationship, seeing Kathryn and Scott made her (and everyone else who saw them) feel otherwise.

Scott smiled and planted another kiss on Kathryn. "I couldn't agree more. But back to this dead person you're talking to. What is this all about? Did she say what she wanted?"

Kathryn jumped in, "Yes, we've got all of those details honey. But now we need to come up with a plan. Daniel's mother has been giving Shelby messages for the past four weeks. And when Shelby gave Daniel the first message, he freaked out. Now the mother is saying Shelby needs to go to Maui with him tomorrow and Shelby has no idea what to do."

Scott stood, arms crossed, head down, legs at a wide stance, contemplating the situation. He and Kathryn were both extremely fascinated by mystical experiences and believed strongly in the afterlife. But neither of them had ever encountered a situation like this before.

"Have you tried connecting with her again to see if she can give you more specifics about how she wants you to do this?"

"Great question," Shelby said. "Right as she was leaving, I asked how I was supposed to bring this up to Daniel, since he totally shut down and didn't contact me for two-and-a-half weeks the last time I delivered one of her messages. She said she would, and I quote, 'take care of it.' But who knows what that even means. If she appeared to Daniel, he would probably lose his mind, which is most likely why she is coming to me instead."

"Well, I think you should be totally honest with him and tell him what happened," Kathryn said. "That's how Scott and I handle everything. We are completely honest and work through things with complete transparency."

Scott chuckled. "Oh, like when you were going ga-ga over that waiter at Andina after the huge fight we had—you know, when we were trying to figure out our future and when we would go to Hungary?"

Kathryn's face crinkled. "Well, I told you…eventually." Leaning over to Shelby, she whispered, loud enough for Laney to hear, "But, I waited like nine months until I felt like he wouldn't be absolutely appalled by my ridiculous behavior. So, that's actually a good point. He'll think you're nuts. Don't say a word. Ask a lot about the trip, tell him you've always wanted to go, see if he invites you. When do you see him next?"

"I see him tonight for some wine at his place and then tomorrow afternoon for lunch. And I think you're right. If momma wants me to ask him about going, she is going to have to pull out some type of divine intervention Daniel can witness as well. I can't do this all on my own. It's been a week of an amazing-awesome love fest. Inviting myself on this trip would be relationship suicide." Shelby paused. "But you know, she did say that we humans get too wrapped up in timeframes. That keeps sticking with me for some reason."

"Well, she's absolutely right," Scott chimed in. "Time is merely a man-made construct to provide us with the feeling of stability and control. Both of which are, of course, an illusion. But it's an illusion we need to operate in the reality we've created for ourselves here. I knew Kathryn was the woman for me as soon as I saw her. My mind said that was impossible, not to mention insane. And then I began to have all of these dreams about her and got really strong messages that she was The One. Turns out, I was right. You don't need a timeframe when it comes to love. You just need love."

Scott's words were still ringing in Shelby's ears as she drove to meet Daniel for lunch the next day at Bread & Ink Café on Southeast Hawthorne. "You just need love."

But, was what she was feeling really love? Were the synchronicities and messages from the other side (not to mention visits) truly a sign that they were meant to be together? Shelby didn't have a clear answer. But, she did know that if she could surrender and trust the flow of the Universe, the answers would be revealed.

Daniel was sitting at a table outside the café when she walked up. It was a lovely October afternoon, with clear skies and near-perfect temps for a Portland Indian summer. He stood to greet her as she walked up, wrapping his arms around her tightly.

"I'm so glad to see you," he whispered in her ear. "I've been thinking about you all day, especially after our night together. I don't know how I'm going to go two weeks without you."

She ran her fingers through his dark brown hair and sighed. "I know, right? I miss you already."

"I know. Me too," he whispered back.

They sat down at the table and stared back at each other.

"I can't believe, at the same time I meet you, all of this is happening, and I'm leaving for two weeks to go to Maui for a break I've been waiting for, for the past year—or my whole life, really."

"It's wild, right? I'm so excited for you, albeit a little jealous. I've always wanted to go to Maui." Shelby figured it was as good a time as any to try out Kathryn's idea.

"Oh really? Have you traveled much?"

"A bit here and there—Mexico, the U.K., Spain, Brazil, Kauai even—but I feel like there's still a bazillion places I would love to see. Maui is definitely on the list. Will you get to do any sightseeing while you're there?"

"You know, to be honest with you, I'm not sure. Kaley hasn't said much except that she, another agent and some publishers are staying at these villas and she wants to spend time reviewing my novel, talking about possibilities with them and see where it takes us. I'm going with it. I haven't had this much interest shown in anything I've written."

Shelby did her best to keep a smile on her face despite the growing pain in her stomach. There was no way Kaley Hamilton wasn't going to be all over Daniel. He was amazing, and good-looking. And according to the word on the street, the woman practically dry humped any good-looking male author in a 10-mile radius of her.

Instead, she replied, "Wow, sounds like an adventure." She took a big drink of water. "A work adventure, that is. Should we order?" Shelby looked down at her menu as though it were the most interesting thing in the world.

"You okay, Shelby? You seem a little, I don't know…I've just never heard your voice get so high-pitched."

"Oh, was it?" Shelby realized it was. "I'm sorry, Daniel. I'm so excited you are having such an awesome break in your career, but I'm a little bummed that you'll be gone for two weeks when I was really starting to get used to you."

"I know," he reached across the table and grabbed her hand. "I am having mixed feelings about going too. In fact, I had the weirdest thing happen when we were at the gardens the other night. I randomly had this thought pop into my head that said, "take Shelby with you." Daniel laughed, more loudly than usual. "I mean, isn't that silly? We just met, like what—a month ago? And we just started spending all our time together this week." He sighed, taking a big drink of water. "Yeah, we should probably order."

Shelby couldn't believe it—he *had* thought about them going to Maui together, as well. Maybe his mom was orchestrating some divine intervention.

The waitress came over to take their order and, out of sheer discomfort with the whole situation, Shelby decided to dive right in and order. I'll take the pepper bleu burger, no bun and please add fries." She caught Daniel looking at her smiling. "I'm starving."

In truth, her stomach was doing a flip-flopping dance inside of her. Was he going to ask her? Wasn't he? Was Kaley Hamilton going to attack him? Is that why his mom wanted her to go with him? Was the life she needed to save Daniel's? Instead of addressing any of those things, she overcompensated by over-ordering in the hopes of acting as though everything was a-okay.

"You know, I'm not that hungry. I'll take your cup of soup and salad."

Apparently Daniel didn't over-order when he wasn't feeling well.

"Oh, well now I feel like a cow. Literally." Shelby grinned.

"No, don't. My head is going in so many directions right now, it's tough to think about food." He squeezed her hand and gave her a faux smile. Shelby realized then that he was doing his best to put on a good face, too.

Their meal passed without incident, as they talked about his book, his trip and Shelby's long-held desire to start her own jewelry business. She had thought about getting a booth at Last Thursday—a street fair on Northeast Alberta—to see how her jewelry did for the upcoming summer, but there never seemed to be any time to research the idea or see about booths at the winter markets. Since meeting Daniel, the inspiration to expand her jewelry's reach was hitting her hard. Lately, she had spent time at work trolling Etsy.com to see how her jewelry might do with an online store. Daniel was incredibly encouraging, telling her to go for it and sharing his experience with quitting his job in radio to focus full-time on his novel. It was inspiring. Shelby almost felt like she could do it. And with Daniel gone for the next two weeks with the seductress-slash-agent Kaley Hamilton, she anticipated that she was going to be making *a lot* of jewelry.

After lunch, they walked down Hawthorne, stopping at Swirl for some fro-yo. Over a cup of tart and pistachio frozen yogurt, Daniel shyly asked, "So...is it okay if I call you while I'm in Maui? I've always wondered what it would be like to have a briefly long-distance love affair and get exorbitant charges on my cell bill. We could try it out."

Shelby giggled, only slightly wondering if a "love affair" was a long-term or short-term commitment in Daniel's mind. "Well, I would love to be part of your ridiculously high cell charges. But seriously, that could cost you an arm and possibly a leg."

"I know, I'm not quite sure how you'll reimburse me. But really, I would love to stay in touch with you while I'm away. We could Skype even. Although that's kind of lame, but a possibility. Since I met you everything in my life has changed, and even though it's only been a week of spending time together, it's been incredible. I guess I'm kind of worried that things might change while I'm gone," Daniel looked down, seemingly interested in the tiles on the floor.

"I'm a bit worried, too. I just…I don't…I'm not sure…I, well, I don't trust Kaley Hamilton," Shelby blurted out. She hadn't meant to say it, but she couldn't help it. Why wasn't Daniel tuned in to Kaley's true motives? Why was this trip happening right as they were falling in love? Daniel looked surprised.

"What do you mean you don't trust her? She's a literary agent for crying out loud." Daniel's voice had an edge of exasperation to it.

"I've heard a few things here and there about her, which has led me to believe that she isn't exactly the most trustworthy woman."

Shelby let her voice trail off, afraid to look directly at Daniel, unsure of how he would respond. She continued, realizing she needed to give him more details, so she didn't sound like a total jealous not-girlfriend, girlfriend. He simply stared back at her blankly, his eyes as big as saucers.

"I mean, I don't for sure know details about anything, but I've heard that she has had romantic liaisons with several of her authors. Her offer to have you come down to Maui is thrilling, but with how good-looking, charming and amazing you are," Shelby was hoping some stroking of Daniel's ego might soften the impact of her message. "I can't help but wonder if she has other motives."

Shelby was back-peddling now, but doing the best she could. She silently cursed her big mouth. Why couldn't she have kept quiet about all of this? He was angry, she could see it in on his face now. The mood had gone from one of connection and love to ego and anger. Shelby felt like she had to back-up her comments, which after saying she didn't trust a woman she didn't know, was necessary. And Daniel's ego wasn't about to let anyone hint that his big-break trip was anything other than his big break.

"Well I appreciate your concern, but I can assure you that nothing even remotely romantic or flirtatious has occurred between Kaley and I. Even her emails to me about this retreat have been all business." Daniel took a big bite of his fro-yo to stall. He was confused by what Shelby was telling him, and upset that she would insinuate that something besides him receiving a big break in his career was occurring. "Do you normally feel jealous in your relationships?"

This lit a fire under Shelby. She was simply trying to warn the guy before he arrived at the lioness' lair.

"Okay Daniel, let's be clear here—this is *not* about me being jealous, but rather me giving you a heads-up on what you might potentially be stepping into. This woman is a known seducer of her authors, and so excuse me for being concerned when she invites a man I'm totally falling for to Maui for two weeks to be with her. And then you tell me that she is being vague with details. Well, I wonder why Daniel? Most likely because the only details she has in mind are getting into bed with you." Shelby knew she was overreacting, but she couldn't stop herself. She was falling *in love* with Daniel and now he was going to Maui and, despite his mother's nudging, Shelby wasn't going with him. What if she lost him for good?

Daniel's jaw tightened. Shelby was raising her voice and people were starting to notice. He stood up.

"Shelby, let's take this outside where we won't cause a scene," he said through gritted teeth.

"My pleasure," Shelby retorted. She was angry. First at

herself for saying something—she had almost made it the whole way through without uttering a word of Kaley's potentially vile motives—and secondly, she was angry that Daniel was so defensive.

As they walked down the sidewalks of Hawthorne, Daniel and Shelby didn't say a word to each other. The tension between them was thick as Shelby cursed herself and his reaction, while Daniel's mind spun. Why was Shelby acting so crazy? There was no chance Kaley was interested in anything more than his book *Shannon Town*. What was going on?

When they finally arrived at the car, Daniel spoke, turning to face Shelby.

"I'm sorry you don't trust Kaley Hamilton. But I do ask that you trust me. I know what I'm doing here, okay?"

As Daniel boarded Hawaiian Air flight 11, he wasn't sure if he knew anything. When he allowed himself to reflect on the possibilities for his book *Shannon Town*, as well as the opportunity to spend two weeks in Maui, he was thrilled. But, that's where the joy stopped. The rest of it felt heavy. His argument with Shelby kept replaying in his mind. How could she act like that? How could she insinuate that this wasn't a huge opportunity for him? And why did he keep feeling what he could only describe as a nudge to have Shelby with him in Maui, even though he wasn't sure how that would go— especially since their fro-yo blow-up?

When he dropped Shelby off, they had kissed briefly, although Shelby was barely able to make eye contact with him. He didn't feel good about how things ended before he left, but he had been so frustrated that he couldn't summon the energy to make things better. As Daniel buckled into his coach seat for the five-hour flight ahead, he couldn't help but imagine what his life might be like when he was flying back home. And what would come of him and Shelby? He honestly wasn't sure.

Daniel put on his headphones to distract himself from the heavy feeling in his body. Radiohead's "Everything In Its Right

Place" came on and Daniel let his mind drift to Maui, to *Shannon Town*, Shelby, Kaley Hamilton, and all that lay before him.

The next thing he knew, a woman was shaking him.

"Sir, sir—we've landed in Maui. It's time to get off the plane."

Daniel rubbed his eyes, coming back to his reality with a start. He looked up at the woman and around him—the plane was empty. Somehow he had slept through the entire flight and missed the landing. All he could remember were brief visions of his dreams—it was like someone had drugged him. There were visions of his mother's face looking down sweetly at him, he and Shelby dancing in white on a beach and, for some odd reason, a wispy outline of a woman dancing around with them. Daniel rubbed his eyes again, trying to wake himself more fully. He felt as though he had completely left his body and traveled somewhere else.

"I'm so sorry, for some reason I completely conked out. Thank you for waking me."

"No problem, sir," the young Hawaiian stewardess replied. "Sometimes coming to the islands puts you in touch with a different reality. Happens all the time."

Daniel looked up at her curiously. She simply smiled, turned and headed to the back of the plane. He thought her remark quite odd, but couldn't give it much thought. He had a meeting with Kaley Hamilton after he checked in. And he wanted to make sure he wasn't drooling with sleep in his eyes. He had to make every moment of the trip count if he wanted his career to be anything like Steinbeck's.

Daniel had never been to Maui before and found himself utterly intoxicated with the palm trees, the sultry warmth, and the smell of hibiscus flowers everywhere. He felt so in love with the area that he upgraded to a Chevrolet Camaro convertible, so he could fully enjoy the energy and scenery of Maui. Kaley Hamilton and friends were staying in a small condominium complex in Kihei about a half hour from the airport. The plan was that Daniel would get settled in (the group was at the Grand Wailea spa for most of the day), and they would all meet up in the courtyard for beverages and appetizers in the early evening.

It was only 2 p.m., so Daniel had a few hours before he had to be "on" to see Kaley and company (which is what he decided he would now call the crew that Kaley had only vaguely referred to). They had exchanged a few emails to set up the schedule and travel arrangements, but Kaley had not been very forthcoming about what type of meetings he should prepare for.

"Don't worry about preparing anything Daniel. We'll keep it all very organic—it is Hawaii after all. We'll see how it unfolds and if Shannon Town might be a fit for any of my publisher friends." Was all she had said via email.

The use of the words "very organic" made Daniel uncomfortable. Whenever people wanted to keep things organic, it usually meant there was zero plan. But, he couldn't imagine that Kaley Hamilton became an agent of such notoriety without planning these types of occasions. Although...with Shelby's allegations about Kaley's motives hanging in the air, Daniel wasn't sure what to believe. But, his mind argued, the fact that she felt his manuscript was quality enough to even be present at this gathering with publishers was a huge compliment to him.

He had been dreaming about this moment for quite some time. And he hoped that if things were too "organic" he could nudge them back into line, a line that included him signing on the dotted line to have his novel published for the entire world to see. He had worked hard to get to this point, and he would be damned if he frittered it away with an "organic" two weeks of being in front of major players in the publishing industry, including Kaley Hamilton.

As he pulled up to the complex he would be staying at for the next two weeks, Daniel was impressed. It appeared to be about 12 units, two levels, formed in a "U" shape with a beautiful courtyard in the middle. The complex was light yellow in color and the grounds were beautifully landscaped with palm, mango, and avocado trees, along with brightly colored flowers of every shape and size. Hibiscus flowers in yellow, purple, and white lined the entire courtyard. In the middle sat a sparkling swimming pool (that looked so good, Daniel wanted to dive right in), two picnic tables, and a large barbeque. In the far corner between two palm trees was a green-and-white hammock.

"They thought of everything," Daniel mumbled under his breath. He looked over at his empty passenger seat and couldn't help but imagine Shelby sitting there, taking all of this in with him. Just thinking of her made him want to connect with her in some way, but he didn't know what to say or do since their last exchange. He decided to send her a quick, generic text: *Just got 2 Maui—it's gorgeous. Will call soon. XO*

Daniel grabbed his bags and headed up to the complex. Kaley had FedEx-ed the key for his room, so all he had to do was unpack his stuff and relax before everyone showed up. He opened the door to room 11 and stood in awe. It was a simple studio, but it had such a luscious Hawaiian feel with an authentic island theme that it took Daniel everything he had not jump up and down on the bed like a little boy. Spending two weeks in paradise was a complete gift from the gods to Daniel. Since his trip to London right before his mother passed on 11 years ago, Daniel had not traveled. It was as though the guilt of leaving when she needed him the most paralyzed him from ever leaving again. Only the prospect of finally doing something his mother would be proud of—to be a published author—could motivate him to travel yet again. And that's why it was so important to him to have an agent and publisher choose him, rather than self-publish. He needed the validation, not just for himself, but for all the years he spent beating himself up about not doing right by his mother.

Standing in the middle of what would be his home for the next two weeks, Daniel took a good look around, grinning from ear to ear. He had done it. This trip was going to change his life—he could feel it. There was a small sitting area with a white, purple and green floral couch with wicker accents, a coffee table, a queen-sized bed with a beautiful floral bedspread, a small tiki brown desk, and a kitchenette with breakfast bar and two wicker stools. The studio was decorated with all purple, green and white, and soft brown wicker accents throughout. It was then that Daniel noticed a large bouquet of flowers and a floral lei on the breakfast bar. He set down his bags and walked over to the card sitting in front of the bouquet.

Welcome to Maui Daniel! I'm so excited you could be here to share in the Aloha spirit. Love, Kaley

Love? Aloha spirit? Odd. Daniel tried not to overthink it. She was a professional, and maybe being in Hawaii just made her more relaxed. Maybe she didn't want to be overly focused on business. *Except that's why I'm here*, he thought. He had tried and had been successful to not put too much pressure on this trip (and the time with Shelby certainly made things much easier, until the fro-yo incident), but now that he was here, simmering in the loveliness of Hawaii, he couldn't help but feel a sense of urgency. A sense of, *c'mon let's do this*. It was like his adrenaline and testosterone were combining into a crazy-motivated cocktail. He was going to have to find a way to take the edge off. He was in Maui, he needed to relax.

Daniel walked into the bathroom, noting that yet again purple, green and white dominated the color scheme. He smiled when he saw the deep bathtub. *Shelby would love to soak in this*, he thought. He imagined her, her hair piled high on top of her head, relaxing in the tub, while Daniel brought her a glass of wine with "Sea and Cake" playing in the background. He would love to sit there with her and talk about anything at all, laugh with her and then, of course, help her get out of the tub and into something more comfortable…

Right then a text came through his phone. It was Shelby.

So glad u made it! Text pics whenever u can. Thinking of u! Xo

Daniel immediately took a photo of the room and the bathtub and texted them to Shelby, with a few x's and o's.

It was after hitting "send" that Daniel felt a pain in his chest. He breathed into it, noticing that it felt like regret. *I shouldn't have let our last time together be an argument. Maybe her intentions were solely out of concern and not jealously. I should have tried harder to make it better or understand her point of view. And I should have asked her to come here with me.* But, the fact of the matter was that all the should's in the world weren't going to change anything. What was done, was done. If Daniel had any chance of pulling off a successful first meeting with Kaley and company, he was going to have to focus on the task at hand. He sat down at the breakfast bar, pulled his manuscript out of his suitcase and started thumbing through it. It was a good book. It would be published. He could feel it.

A slight breeze drifted in through the window and the smell of the islands made him relax. He had to trust that everything was happening as it was meant to. What transpired over the next two weeks could set his career on fire and bring even more meaning to his life. He needed to keep his focus positive, so that what he wanted—Kaley Hamilton to represent his work, securing him a lucrative book deal and for his work to reach mainstream America—could take place. Then, he could see where things with Shelby would go next.

He was a man with a plan.

Daniel checked the time, noting he had about an hour-and-a-half before he needed to be clean-shaven and ready to meet Kaley. He thought about lying down for a nap, but he wasn't tired. He had slept the entire five-hour flight and felt energized. He decided to go for a short walk down to the beach to experience the island manna for the first time himself. He also wanted to take some photos to send to Shelby.

As he walked down to the beach, he was overcome with a strong sense of gratitude and joy. It was true that this past year hadn't gone the way he would have liked. But, it had allowed him to finish his novel, and it had led him to the Willamette Writers Conference where he met Shelby—and meeting her had inspired him so much creatively and personally that he had nailed the pitch with Kaley. Because of that, he was here, at one of the most beautiful places on earth to meet publishers and discuss his book. He had spent the past week with one of the most beautiful, smart, amazing and sexy women he had ever met. When Shelby touched him, his whole body melted.

He flashed back to their last night before the lunch time fro-yo incident. Shelby had been wearing a sexy turquoise-blue halter dress that was slightly formfitting. With a glass of wine in hand, she had walked over to him as he was sitting on the couch, a look of intensity in her eyes. He could see it so clearly even now—it was like he was experiencing the moment all over again. She set her wine down and sat on top of him, her legs straddling his body. He had put his hands on her thighs, gripping them firmly as she leaned down to kiss him, her tongue tempting him. As his hands dug into her thighs, she let her hands linger all over his body, his face, his neck, stopping to kiss his ears, her tongue gently licking him as her hot breath sent chills up his spine. She sat up at that moment, her hands on his face looking at him and said, "You're amazing. Don't ever forget that. I am so blessed to be sharing this moment with you."

Daniel was so overcome with emotion that he grabbed her, pulling her into him, kissing her so powerfully it took his breath away. His hands covered every inch of her body; he had to feel her in every way he could. Then, she pulled away again, kneeling down in front of him. Her eyes looked up into his as she slowing began to unbutton his pants, taking her time, never breaking their gaze. Daniel's heart rate increased and his breath turned heavy. He wanted her, all of her and he could feel she wanted him.

"Sync your breath up with mine," she said softly as she began stroking him. Daniel did as she asked without question. She was a goddess to him and in this moment he would follow whatever she asked. As they kept their gazes fixed on one another, breathing in unison, Daniel felt energy swirling in his root chakra at the base of his spine. He could feel it growing larger as it swirled, the intensity of his pleasure rising beyond anything he had ever experienced before.

"Hey! Watch out idiot!" a driver yelled at Daniel, blaring his horn.

Daniel was so enmeshed in remembering that night with Shelby that he had almost walked right into oncoming traffic. The connection between he and Shelby was so overpowering, it was even affecting his ability to function when she wasn't around. Daniel had to remind himself why he was in Maui in the first place. This was his big break, one that he wanted to be fully present for. Day-dreaming about his time with Shelby would have to be reserved for a later date.

"And yee-ah, and yee-ah!"

Shelby yelled along with the other women in the StudioNia classroom, following the petite instructor Trixie's every move. Trixie was Shelby's favorite instructor—with short auburn brown locks, dazzling green eyes and the best taste in workout fashion Shelby had ever seen. Shelby had been practicing Nia for several years, being particularly drawn to it because she both loved dance and being able to get her anger out with a yell every now and again.

Nia was a dance class that combined elements of martial, dance, and healing arts all together. It was also the only workout class where she could get dressed up and sweat. Today, she was wearing a short, multicolored tank dress over capri leggings, earrings, and her heart charm necklace. She tried to get Kathryn's attention to see how she was doing (she had only been to Nia a couple of times prior). But Kathryn—who had been overtaken by a Nia clothing sale and was now covered in head-to-toe purple lycra—didn't notice, she was so intently following Trixie. Kathryn had actually been the one to convince Shelby that what she needed was a good sweat session at Nia after the argument with Daniel, balancing her masculine and feminine aspects to make her forget about what might potentially happen now that he was in Maui with Kaley Hamilton. Shelby had agreed only because she had spent the past day since he left feeling very uneasy.

Why hadn't she said she was sorry? She didn't know Kaley Hamilton. Everything she had heard through *Hello Portland* about Kaley were simply rumors. And even if it were true, it wasn't her place to tell Daniel about it. He needed to figure things out for himself. Shelby wanted to go to Daniel, wrap her arms around him and tell him how sorry she was. But now he was in Maui, and there was nothing more that could be done.

"You're not in control. Whatever is meant to happen, will happen," Kathryn had reminded her. And she knew that, but it didn't stop the gnawing in her gut.

When Daniel sent the text that he had arrived and the place was gorgeous, she couldn't help but feel a bit melancholy. She wanted to be there with him.

As Celine Dion belted out:
"There were nights when the wind was so cold
That my body froze in bed
If I just listened to it
Right outside the window"

Shelby found herself getting lost in the music, her body somehow effortlessly following Trixie's.

"But when you touch me like this
And you hold me like that
I just have to admit
That it's all coming back to me"

Her body shivered as she flashed back briefly to her last full night with Daniel before their argument. The heat of his breath on her neck, the way his hands knew exactly how to touch her, the smell of him on top of her—it was as if the Universe had created him just for her. She felt the stirring in her yoni, and she tried to refocus her attention on her dancing.

They hadn't had sex—although Shelby felt they had definitely made love—because they both agreed 1) they had plenty of time for that, and 2) they wanted to be wholly and fully committed to one another before they took that step. Shelby had stopped having sex without a deep and meaningful connection after her early twenties. She noticed that when she had sex without a meaningful connection, it felt like a violation to her body in some way. That somehow her body knew that no man should enter her unless their connection was fully in alignment as spiritual and physical beings. It was something she simply knew. It felt wrong to have a man inside of her when it wasn't the man she felt she was absolutely meant to be with in that moment. Daniel seemed to understand—sharing that he too was done with careless sex and was seeking a more meaningful connection on all levels before moving into anything more.

But, that didn't mean it was easy for them not to go there. Their chemistry was full-on passion, meaning they had to be mindful of their intentions when it came to penetration in those heated moments. And Shelby knew that in the back of her mind was the uncertainty of what would happen once Daniel returned in two weeks. His life could potentially be totally different. For now, she had to do her best not to spend too much time worrying about Kaley Hamilton, while still allowing herself to lust after Daniel. Not the easiest thing in the world for a girl to do.

After the Nia class, she and Kathryn grabbed a coffee at Case Study Coffee, and then decided to head down to the Saturday Market.

"So, did it help?" Kathryn asked, as she pulled her brown curls back into a ponytail.

"It did, until that damn Celine Dion song, that is."

"Oh man, I know. When you touch me like this, when you hold me like that. I was doing my best not to get all worked up about Scott right then and there."

"I know, right?"

"Amen, sister!"

They high-fived and giggled. Scott had come up with this ridiculous yet catchy word rule that whenever someone said, "Right?"—and in Portland that happened often —it had to be followed with an "Amen."

"But seriously," Shelby continued. "The chemistry between us is so off the charts, it's taken everything I've got to not sleep with him. I just couldn't before he went to see Kaley Hamilton, anyway."

"Sweetie, Kaley Hamilton can be as big of a cougar as she wants to be, but if Daniel feels it like how you're feeling it, you've got nothing to worry about. And you know, I've got to remind you, what we think about we bring about, so stop manifesting that Kaley the lioness is going to devour your guy."

"I know, you're right. I've got to shake this negativity. It's not good for me and it's not helping the Universe deliver to me what I want either."

"Speaking of non-physical deliveries, have you heard anything more from his mom?"

"No, she's been pretty quiet. For some reason, I feel like she's there in Maui with Daniel. I know she's trying to help him and something about our connection has opened him up more. I'm hoping she'll be giving the messages exclusively to him from now on. And I hope she isn't too angry that I didn't follow her wacky advice to invite myself to Maui. Whoever's life had to be saved, will have to be saved by her or someone else. I did the best I could," Shelby shrugged, unsure of what more she could say or do.

"Well, you've got to admit, it's pretty cool that you were communicating with a non-physical being on the other side. Whether or not she was sort of a nag."

The two of them laughed, as they made their way down to the Saturday Market.

As they entered the market, the smell of caramel corn and chicken kabobs filled the air. They both looked over at one another and said in unison, "Food!" and quickly headed over to the part of the market where all of the food vendors were located. It was a nice crisp October day, and already vendors were doling out holiday wares—both for Halloween and Christmas. All of that goodness would have to wait while Shelby and Kathryn ate. Shelby found a chicken tamale at Dona Lola's and wandered over to where the tables were while Kathryn searched for something she could eat that followed all of her various food restrictions. Shelby was grateful that she could eat whatever she wanted within reason. She practiced yoga a few times a week and went on hikes on the weekend, and that seemed to fit her body perfectly.

Shelby found a couple of seats and sat down to take in the scene while waiting for Kathryn. An older woman in a corner booth caught her attention. The woman was dressed in a simple white top and a long pink-and-white skirt, her golden hair streaked with gray and pulled back into a low bun at the nape of her neck. She was looking right at Shelby, her face well-lined with what looked like years of a fascinating life. Shelby could not stop looking at her. Her booth was nondescript, but for whatever reason, Shelby had to go talk to her. She stood up, leaving her tamale on the table, and walked over to the strange woman.

"Well, hello there," the woman said in a thick Croatian accent.

"I'm sorry for staring, but I couldn't look away."

"You were called. I can see all the angels around you. Come, sit here." The woman patted the chair in front of her.

"Are you a psychic or an intuitive?"

The woman smiled slightly.

"I am simply a woman who knows things. The people who are drawn to me are the people who I am meant to share this gift with."

Shelby was still standing. Was this just some ploy to make money? She looked around for Kathryn, but she was nowhere to be found.

"I—I have a friend," she turned and looked around again, pointing.

"It's no use, you will not find her. Your angels are directing you now, especially this one woman who has a very strong presence with you."

Shelby turned back to face the woman, sitting down in front of her.

"There's a woman with me?"

"Yes, she's here on your left, on your feminine side. She's whispering in your ear a lot, encouraging you, giving you messages, warning you too. But you know this already, don't you?"

Shelby swallowed hard. "How much will this cost?"

"Whatever you feel like donating. This is not about money, my dear, this is about sharing my gift. We all have gifts, and it's our responsibility to share them. When we do not, we cripple up and die. I am 88 years old, but you would not have guessed it would you? I use my gift." She smiled broadly now. "And it provides for me everything I have ever wanted. Now, would you like me to continue?"

"Yes, yes please."

"This woman, she is connected to you in some very deep way—maybe past life, maybe karmic—that does not really matter. Right now, what matters is that you hold on to something very important to her. You are entrusted with the care of someone she loves very much. Do you understand?"

"I do. But why am I the one— "

"This is not of your concern dear heart. You are a very powerful soul and your soul agreed long before you came here to come together with this person, and you two would save each other." She grabbed Shelby's hand, turning it palm up, tracing the lines with her other finger. She looked back up at Shelby. "You know that's what love does don't you? It is never accident when this happens. It is always divine and it is always so both souls can ascend to the next level. But you..." The woman clucked her tongue. "You and this other are stubborn. Think you know it all already. His heart is broken when this woman left, yes? And you, you keep yourself so busy so you don't have to feel the love, even though it courses through your veins."

Tears began to stream down Shelby's face.

"This woman is a gift to you and to the other. She is a guide for you on the path. Listen to her. Follow whatever she says."

"Even when she says I should fly to Maui uninvited to see him?"

"Yes, even then. She is trying to help you both. She's been

trying for years to bring you together. Now it has happened and divine will is taking place. You two are too independent, too untrusting of love. It will be work, but you must trust the path. Always trust the path."

The woman closed her eyes. She dropped Shelby's hand. When her eyes opened they glowed a spectacular, iridescent gray color.

"You are satisfied?"

Shelby was full of questions, but too shell-shocked to respond. Her entire body was covered in goosebumps as waves of energy rolled through her. She felt Daniel's mother to her left. Now she knew whose lives (as in plural, she suddenly realized!) his mother was referring to being saved. And she felt certain of what she had to do next.

———

Daniel closed the condo door behind him and made his way into the main courtyard to meet up with Kaley and the other publishers. He felt so good; it was as if every cell in his body were vibrating at an abundant level. The walk along the beach had calmed his masculine urgency cocktail into a feeling of peace and assuredness. It had also allowed him to clear his mind of the fro-yo incident, along with the confusing feeling that Shelby should be with him. He was a man on a mission, a mission to make his mother proud and to really be something—a published author.

Freshly shaven, wearing light khaki pants paired with a light blue short-sleeve button down and camel-colored flip-flops (it was Maui after all), Daniel was ready to set the world on fire. He was also ready to pitch the hell out of *Shannon Town* to whomever Kaley put in front of him. He felt it down to his core—it was his time to shine.

As Daniel neared the courtyard, he immediately spotted Kaley. She was wearing a long white sundress and appeared far more tan than Daniel remembered. *She must be able to vacation a lot with all the high-level authors she represents*, Daniel thought. She was surrounded by two other couples, in their late-to mid-forties, all looking quite casual and relaxed with suntanned faces, as they sat in white Adirondack chairs, chatting. A mobile tiki bar sat behind them, along with a table of fresh fruits, skewered meats, and salads.

"Daniel!"

Kaley called after Daniel as soon as he entered the courtyard. She rushed over to him, spreading her arms wide for a hug, lightly kissing him on the cheek.

"We're so glad to have you join us, Daniel. It's going to be a lovely two weeks. Do you love the place already or what?" She smiled at Daniel and then at the others.

"Actually, I do love it. It feels so…so…free. You definitely pick the right places to do business Kaley."

"Oh, Daniel. We're hardly doing business. I mean, look at us!"

Daniel looked around and noticed that by now the other four guests with Kaley had cocktails in hand and were smiling red-faced at both of them.

"Now Daniel, you must meet Jonathan Richer and his wife, Emily. Jonathan works for Penguin Publishing and his wife is an interior designer. She did my place—it's quite fabulous if I do say so myself. And over here is Richard Closterman and his wife, Sarah. Sarah is an associate editor at Tonga Publishing, and her handsome husband is a realtor—he's actually the one who connected me to these magnificent condos."

Daniel shook the couple's hands, trying his best to put together what was happening.

"It's wonderful to meet all of you. And thank you for the hospitality—these condos and the grounds really feel like paradise." Daniel turned to Kaley. "Kaley, can I speak with you for a minute?"

"Oh, of course dear. And Richard will you get Daniel a cocktail? You like Mai Tais right Daniel? It really is the only thing to drink when you're on the islands."

Richard nodded, his large Hawaiian button-up and khaki shorts hanging loosely on his broad 6'2" frame, as he got up and made his way over to the mobile tiki bar to make more cocktails.

Daniel walked to the far corner of the courtyard with Kaley.

"Kaley, um, where is Thomas Berring, your contact at Random House?"

"Oh Daniel. You are all business, aren't you?"

It occurred to Daniel then that Kaley might be intoxicated.

"Well, I did think that's why you asked me over here. So, I'm a little confused, because it seems like I might be merely joining you on vacation with some of your friends."

Kaley smiled.

"Sometimes it's okay to mix business with pleasure, Daniel." She leaned in, touching the collar of his shirt and stroking it lightly. "Besides, Thomas really isn't that much fun to do business or pleasure with," Kaley winked. "So, you're better off that he had a family thing come up and couldn't make it. All you have to do is relax Daniel. We'll work your book into our conversations with Sarah and Jonathan. I already love it, so I know they will too."

She stepped in even closer to Daniel, reaching up to smooth his hair. Daniel could smell the alcohol on her breath—she was clearly drunk. He wasn't quite sure what to do. Perhaps this was how things worked in the publishing industry and if he could keep his cool and go with the flow, maybe things would turn out all right. Or, even worse—perhaps Shelby had been right and Kaley's whole plan for him had nothing to do with his book. Daniel couldn't stand the thought of that, and a huge lump formed in his throat.

"So, to be clear Kaley, we're just going to be hanging out for two weeks in the hopes that a casual mention about my book might catch their attention?"

"They're on vacation Daniel—it's not like we want to barrage them with book talk. They get enough of that back east. And anyway, it gives us a good opportunity to get to know each other better." She was still stroking the collar of his button-down shirt.

Daniel was speechless. It appeared that this incredibly successful agent, who worked with authors all over the world—primarily male authors, he now realized—was making a play for him. Kaley had told him to come to Maui to meet with an "intimate" group of folks from the publishing world to discuss his book *Shannon Town*. In truth, he was now on vacation with Kaley and two couples who were close friends of hers. He had taken out a huge chunk of cash to fly to Maui, all in the hopes that this might be his big break. He felt like an idiot. Shelby *was* right. What would he tell people back home when he returned?

"Daniel, don't worry," Kaley turned serious. "Your book will get picked up. Just have some fun, okay?"

Daniel took a step back, unhinging Kaley from his clothes and personal space.

"Kaley, I'm having trouble understanding what is going on here. So, I will do my best to relax and spend time with your friends, but we're going to talk more about my book—you and me anyway—tomorrow when you're…" Daniel's voice trailed off. "Tomorrow when it's a fresh, new day."

"Oh, a man who tells me what to do. I like that!" Kaley cooed and began walking back to join the others.

Daniel shook his head as he walked back behind her. What had he gotten himself into? A small voice whispered Shelby's name and he looked up suddenly. Shelby was not going to be impressed with this situation at all, in addition to knowing that she had been right. He didn't want to admit how naïve he had been. The whole situation made a Mai Tai sound really, really good. Maybe a few of those would make it easier for him to admit that he was so eager to make his dreams comes true that he was willing to believe just about anything anyone in the industry said—including a highly successful and attractive literary agent.

Richard handed Daniel a cocktail as he sat down in one of the open chairs.

"Thanks Richard—I really need this right about now."

"I hear that, and fortunately you've come to the right place. Kihei is the ideal place to get away from it all."

"I second that!" cheered Sarah sitting casually in one of the chairs, her dark black hair pulled back into a ponytail, comfortably dressed in white gaucho pants with a turquoise top.

"So Daniel, if you're here with Kaley, we can only assume you too are in the writing biz," said Jonathan with a slight British accent. "What project are you working on these days?" Jonathan seemed the most grounded of the group so far to Daniel, as he sat with an air of confidence—his bald head shining in the dusk of the evening—next to his wife Emily (who, by the way, Daniel noticed could have easily passed as a model, her caramel locks perfectly blown out to match her caramel skin, wearing a pink tank and denim short-shorts. She looked to be about 10 years Jonathan's junior.).

Daniel caught Kaley out of the corner of his eye smiling broadly.

"Well, Jonathan, it's funny you should ask, as Kaley and I were only minutes earlier discussing this very topic. In fact, Kaley invited me down here so I could connect with you all more about my novel, *Shannon Town*."

"Kaley, you did not!" Sarah squealed. "We're on vacation!"

Daniel thought he saw Kaley frown, but she quickly smiled. "Now, you know I would never interfere with our vacation unless it was for a very good cause."

The others laughed.

"Daniel has written an incredible historical fiction novel that has a slight western edge to it. And of course, I think every one of you should read it—that means Emily and Richard, too."

Richard and Emily rolled their eyes, obviously familiar with Kaley's habit of bringing work into their social gatherings.

"I also thought it would be really good for Daniel to get out of rainy Portland for inspiration, and also so that he and I could discuss more seriously what our working relationship will be." Kaley smiled seductively over at Daniel. "Either way, everyone wins. We're in Maui, we've got a never-ending stream of Mai Tais coming our way and we're surrounded by lovely, gifted people. Who could want anything more?"

Everyone raised their glasses to toast. Daniel joined in, shrugging his shoulders. Kaley was good, he had to hand it to her. It seemed as though she could make just about any situation work in her favor.

———

After three Mai Tais, Daniel was feeling so good and having such a great time that he forgot that Kaley had essentially tricked him into coming to Maui. He was getting along great with Richard and Sarah, who also had a strong love of the Pacific Northwest (they had a house in Seattle's trendy Capitol Hill area), good coffee, and great reads.

Daniel stumbled up to his room around 1 a.m., bidding the others goodnight and ignoring Kaley's lengthy stares his way. He thought for a second that he saw something move in his room as he put the key in the door, but forgot all about it as he lay down on his comfy bed.

———

Daniel, Daniel. A woman's voice was whispering in Daniel's ear.

Daniel, can you hear me?

He opened his eyes slowly, and saw a sprinkle of lights above his head.

Over here Daniel.

The woman's voice was closer in his ear now. And she was holding his hand.

Daniel looked over and bolted upright in his bed.

"Jesus Christ!"

Daniel, listen to me, I have something to tell you—

"Jesus Fucking Christ! What are you doing here? What is going on? I can't see this, what are you doing?"

Daniel, please calm down, she said, this time a bit louder. *This is important.*

"This cannot be happening. This is not you. You're—you're—dead!"

Daniel's mother smiled, although her face was more blurred than the rest of her. Daniel could feel her soft skin holding his hand gently. He could smell her smell, the smell only she had. It was a mixture of ivory with moth balls. He wasn't sure why moth balls, but it just was—it was how his mom smelled.

Daniel, I am no longer in physical form, yes—

"This is *not* happening. Do you hear me? This is not happening. I can't see you like this, I can't, I'm sorry, I can't. I can't handle this."

Daniel was 100 percent freaked out. He couldn't breathe. His mind was racing trying to make sense of what he was seeing. She was standing right beside him. It was her and he couldn't believe that it was her. It didn't make sense. She had to leave. He needed her to leave. She could not stay.

"You have to go, mom, you have to go! Please go. I'm sorry," Tears now streamed down Daniel's face. "I can't, I can't do this. Please go. Please go." Daniel put his hands to his face and sobbed.

Shhh...love. It's going to be all right. He felt her hand softly rub his back.

Then, he felt a slight breeze of cold air at the foot of the bed. His tears stopped and he looked over to the right where she had been standing. Only she was gone.

For some reason, Daniel now felt calm and sleepy. He laid back down, his mind somehow detaching from what had only moments before occurred, his body heavy, aching for the support of the bed. Immediately, he drifted off into a deep sleep. And there, he saw his mother. This time he did not feel afraid. It was only a dream and he couldn't feel or smell her the way he had before. He was safe now.

"Daniel, there's something you must know." This time, his mother wasn't whispering. They were sitting in the living room where he had grown up, and it felt like the most natural thing in the world that they were talking.

"Yes, mom, what is it?"

"Shelby is the girl you're meant to spend your life with." She looked at him pointedly, neither smiling nor frowning. She had always been good like that—able to deliver any news with such grace.

Daniel simply nodded.

"I want you to fly her over here to be with you. Call her tomorrow and tell her about my visit. She will understand and she will come to you. It's time now, Daniel. I didn't want to get overly involved before, and thought giving you both little hints would be enough. But, you're both far too stubborn and independent. So, here I am. You cut yourself off from me energetically by blaming yourself for my physical transition. I couldn't reach you, your energy was so heavy and so filled with self-loathing and grief. Shelby was the opening, so I could connect with you again. The fact is Daniel, you have an important destiny to fulfill here in this lifetime and Shelby is a big part of that. You two need each other."

His mother got up off the couch and Daniel stood up with her. She wrapped her arms around him and whispered gently in his ear, "And I *am* so proud of you. You have become a wonderful man."

The birds chirping outside his window woke Daniel up. He could still feel her arms wrapped around him and the beauty of her words. Tears streamed down his face, and although he attempted to wipe them away, they kept flowing. It was as if he had been crying all night in his sleep. Daniel rubbed his eyes as the details of the night became clearer to him.

His mother, his dead mother, had visited him from the other side. And while she had tried to give him a message in-person, because he wasn't able to handle that type of communication, she penetrated his dream and gave him the message that way. Either way, what had occurred was real, Daniel could not deny that. His mind drifted briefly to Shelby, and how he had reacted so negatively by pushing her away when she shared the messages she was receiving from his mom, as well as when she warned him about Kaley. Now, he knew without a shadow of a doubt, that it was true. Shelby wasn't trying to soothe his pain out of her care for him, she was actually communicating with his mom, who was now communicating with him. Shelby only had his best interests at heart.

That stewardess had been right, Daniel thought. Visiting the islands *did* put him in touch with another reality. A reality in which the veil between the physical and the non-physical was almost non-existent.

"Housekeeping."

A knock on the door surprised Daniel. He had opened the windows and was letting the sun pour in, but had not been able to venture outside. From the moment he opened his eyes, he had this unquenchable desire to…write. He had been at his laptop for two hours and could not stop.

The knocking came again.

Daniel got up and opened the door, dressed only in board shorts, his chiseled chest and six-pack abs fully exposed.

"Sorry, I don't need any housekeeping— "

"Well Daniel, I don't think there's any housekeeping at the condos, but tea service is as close as you're gonna get."

Kaley Hamilton stood in front of him dressed in a coral halter dress and wedge sandals, along with a tray of tea, scones, and fresh fruit.

"May I come in?

"Actually Kaley, I am really into something right now. I woke up with the storyline for my next novel and I haven't been able to stop writing."

"Listen Daniel, I'm really sorry about last night. I would like to spend some time later today together to talk more. We're all going out on the boat snorkeling if you'd like to join us."

"You know Kaley, I'm feeling inspired and want to focus on my writing. But thanks so much for bringing me tea."

Daniel grabbed the tray and shut the door. He didn't have time for Kaley's antics this morning. He had writing to do.

It was right around 2 p.m. when Daniel stopped writing. He had spent six hours glued to his laptop. And now, he was famished, yet exhilarated. He had never written anything like what was pouring out of him, but he couldn't stop. He was shocked that what was coming out onto the page appeared to be a historical romance novel. Whatever was happening was not something he was painstakingly crafting, it was coming through him. Daniel had never had this type of experience with writing before. Typically, it was pretty painful and anxiety producing. He usually agonized over the plot and where to take it next. He had experienced that few days before the Willamette Writers Conference, when things were flowing well for him, but it wasn't even comparable to what he was feeling now. The words flowed out of Daniel and it felt like he was remembering a story he already knew—almost as if he was re-creating a story he had known long ago.

Daniel threw on a shirt and walked outside. Kaley and her crew had already departed and, other than the distant sound of the ocean and palm trees blowing in the wind, the world around him was quiet. He took a deep breath of the floral air and sighed. He had never felt this at peace before.

Just then, he felt his phone vibrate in his shorts pocket. It was Shelby.

Had MOST amazing reading from a psychic @ Saturday Mkt. Can't wait 2 tell u bout it! Xo

Shelby. Daniel had let himself get so caught up in the novel, he hadn't taken the time to fully process what his mother had shared with him. Hell, he hadn't even had time to fully process the fact that his dead mother had visited him. He needed to tell Shelby. But could he tell her his mother's guidance that they were meant to be together in this lifetime? He wasn't so sure. But, he did need to get her to Maui to be with him. And he did need to let her know she had been right all along. As it turns out, about pretty much everything.

And Kaley Hamilton—what in the world was he going to do with that nutty lady? He didn't care how incredible she appeared to be as an agent, he was so angry that she lured him to Maui under false pretenses. Although there were plenty of upsides to her exaggeration of the truth: it was gorgeous, he really loved Jonathan and Emily, and Richard and Sarah, and somehow Maui had served as a portal for his mother to appear to him. Even so, he didn't feel like he could trust her. Wasn't that exactly what Shelby had said? And she had been right. Daniel knew he could trust Shelby. And he knew he would rather self-publish his books than work with someone who was dishonest. Knowing his mother was proud of him set him free from all of the rules he had created for himself—like the supposition that he was only truly a writer if someone else published his work.

Standing there, looking out over the beauty of Maui, Daniel knew what he had to do.

He picked up his cell phone and dialed Shelby's number.

"So, spare no details—is it as gorgeous as the Internet and game show prize offerings make it out to be?" Shelby's voice was light and full of energy. Daniel immediately felt himself relax; hearing her voice was so soothing to him.

"Well, it's beautiful, but not near as gorgeous as you," Daniel couldn't believe his own cheesiness, but he also couldn't help himself. The last several days were worlds away from the time he spent with Shelby and now he couldn't wait to have her near him again.

"Aren't you Mr. Smooth! What's that Hawaiian air doing to you over there Daniel?"

Daniel chuckled. Shelby truly had no idea what the Hawaiian air was doing to him. But, he was eager to tell her—in person.

"There is definitely something in the air Shelby, and it's incredibly powerful. I really want to tell you all about it…but, I thought it might be a lot better if I told you in person." Daniel paused.

Shelby strained her ears trying to decipher if she had heard him correctly. Was he asking her to come to Maui right now or was she going to have to wait over a week and a half to get the scoop? She remained silent; she wasn't about to risk totally sticking her foot in her mouth—again.

"Shelby, are you there?"

"Yes, I'm here," she said quietly.

"Well...." Daniel took a deep breath; Shelby's silence was making him feel uneasy about what he was about to say next. Perhaps she was still upset after their argument and didn't want to come to Maui. How would he handle that? Daniel wasn't good at vulnerability unless he was certain that it would be reciprocated. But now, he had put it out there, and since the whole thing came via orders mandated by his mother, he had to follow through. As he exhaled, he said, "Would you like to fly to Maui tomorrow and spend the rest of the time with me? I found a flight leaving out of Portland tomorrow at 8:35 a.m. And before you respond, I also want to apologize. You were right—about everything—but more specifically, about Kaley. I'm sorry I didn't trust your intuition more. And I really would love to have you here with me. I regret that I didn't ask you sooner."

Shelby felt goosebumps cover her arms and flow up and down her entire torso. Of course she wanted to go! After Daniel's mother told her she was supposed to go to Maui with him, she had scoped out her available vacation time. As for her boss, she planned to tell him that she had a last-minute opportunity come up that she couldn't turn down. Secretly, she hoped he would fire her, so she could focus on her jewelry business and collect unemployment. But, either way, she was most definitely going to Maui.

Shelby's silence made Daniel more uncertain still, so he continued, "And don't worry about paying for airfare—that's on me. Kaley's business account is paying for the condo, so you're good there, too. Just bring money for shopping and anything else you'd like to do. If you want to go, that is." Daniel was rushing his words now, trying to get it all out. Now that he made up his mind, he could feel the depth of his mother's words. Shelby needed to be there with him. He wasn't sure why, but he just knew she had to be.

"Daniel, of course I'll come meet you in Maui. I would love to." Shelby could barely contain her excitement. "And thank you for your apology, but you have to know that I'm the one who's sorry. It was none of my business. I should have trusted that you knew what you were doing and didn't need my two cents."

"Shelby, let's agree to leave that disagreement in the past. We've each owned our piece, but in the future I want to hear your intuitions. It's my job to learn how to receive them more thoughtfully."

"And my job to be more gentle in my delivery," Shelby chimed in.

"Yes, perfect. So we're settled then?" Daniel was grinning from ear-to-ear. Maybe everything *was* happening exactly as it was meant to.

"It's settled," Shelby said.

"Great! I'll book the ticket and send you the confirmation. Do you think it will be a problem with work?"

"Don't worry about that—I'll take care of it. In fact, while you've been gone, I've had a lot shifting over here. I've got my jewelry line—even though it's just a few pieces, but growing—on Etsy.com and I've got more orders coming in. So, I'm okay if Dillion Turkin fires me for taking a vacation with one day's notice."

Daniel had been so invigorated when he woke up that he didn't fully think through the consequences of Shelby coming to Maui at the last minute. He didn't want to be responsible for something as serious as her losing her job. He remembered how critical it was to receive a regular paycheck before he started writing full-time. It had allowed him to pay off his bills and save up enough money to feel safe to take the plunge. The realities of his plan began to sink in, as his left brain returned to its familiar place of logic and doubt.

"Well, Shelby, please don't do this if it's going to cause problems for you at work. I don't want you to be without your job and a paycheck."

Shelby laughed. "Daniel, I'm a big girl and I know it will all work out. I'm not going to hold you responsible for losing my job."

They hung up the phone with a little tension remaining between them. Daniel worried that somehow he was losing his mind, quite possibly hallucinating his mother's presence and guidance, and now he could be responsible for Shelby losing her perfectly good paying job. What was he thinking just pulling more money out of his dwindling savings to fly her to Maui at the last minute anyway?

His mind had returned with some serious issues around the events of the past 24 hours.

Shelby felt frustrated that Daniel's concern was his alleged responsibility if she lost her job. Their connection was so strong, but he seemed to doubt it often or get pulled into his head whenever they came to a new intersection. Why did he ask her to fly over at the last minute if he was going to get all worried about her job? Shelby shook her head. Sometimes she wondered if she had made the whole thing up—visits from his mother, messages from the other side. Was she actually the crazy one?

7

"Aloha, welcome to Hawaii."

Shelby felt butterflies in her stomach as she walked off the plane and into the Kahului airport. Travelers circled all around her, everyone knowing exactly where they were going, and Shelby feeling confused about her true purpose for being in Maui. Daniel had asked her to come join him, then acted flustered, almost taking back his invitation at the thought of Shelby losing a job she didn't love anyway. To top it off, he hadn't really communicated with her since their conversation yesterday.

What was she doing?

The job had been a non-issue. Her editor actually seemed surprised that she would make such a ballsy move, congratulated her for snagging a guy that could fly her to Maui and then asked her to write a piece about traveling from Portland to Maui. So, she was still gainfully employed, and her jewelry line was continuing to blossom. Now she was on her way to see a man who she felt intuitively was her next partner. But, did he know it? That was the real question. A question Shelby was intent on receiving the answer to on this trip.

"Shelby! Over here."

Shelby turned to see Daniel standing near the baggage claim

area in the open-air portion of the airport. He was smiling. Shelby couldn't help but smile in return. The nagging tension she had felt earlier seemed to disappear.

She walked quickly over to him, her blonde hair being softly tousled as a light Hawaiian breeze blew through the baggage corridors.

"Daniel Tillman."

"Shelby Hanson. I missed you."

Shelby jumped up, wrapping her arms and legs around Daniel. His hands gripped her thighs, his thumbs rubbing them softly. Their lips met in unison and the disconnect, the tension, and the questions all faded away. Daniel's lips enveloped hers and Shelby felt herself sink into his body even further. She didn't care who was watching. This was her man.

"God, I missed you." Daniel sighed into her blonde locks as he held onto her. "The thing is, I didn't even realize how much until right now."

"I know," Shelby whispered back.

She had kept herself busy while Daniel was away, but she had felt their disconnect as soon as the argument happened at the frozen yogurt shop. Now that they were together like this, she felt her strong feelings for him fully met and accepted by him. In this moment, they were unified and on the same page.

As Daniel set Shelby back down, he stroked her face softly.

"Thank you for coming here to be with me. I'm sorry for being such an ass on the phone about your job. I know you know what you're doing and I apologize for indicating anything otherwise. It's sort of ironic, right? Me getting frustrated that you implied that I didn't know what I was doing with Kaley and this publishing retreat, and then you having to deal with me not fully trusting that you knew what you were doing with your job and coming here. Two different sides of the same coin, eh? We just may be the perfect fit."

Shelby's eyes filled with tears. He was not only aware of the dynamic between then, but he was apologizing for his part in it. She couldn't believe how blessed she was to have such an aware man in her life. Not to mention sexy. Shelby didn't know if it was the week apart or the fact that they hadn't had sex yet (probably both), but either way Daniel looked so good she wanted to disrobe him right then and there in the airport. He was wearing blue Bermuda shorts and a white T-shirt with flip-flops—in true Hawaiian style, and absolutely devour-able in Shelby's eyes.

As they walked back to his car, Daniel couldn't take his eyes off of Shelby, which made it rather difficult to walk, carry her bags and direct her to the car. But somehow he did it. She looked stunning in her white sundress, her blonde hair *au natural*, not straightened or curled. Wedge sandals and big tortoiseshell sunglasses made her look like something straight out of a magazine. Her toned legs were also getting a considerable amount of his attention. She was so unbelievably sexy that he couldn't believe he had been able to control himself for over a month now and not make love to her. Maybe this trip would be a turning point for them. Maybe that's why his mother had been so insistent that Shelby be there. Perhaps now that he knew the real deal with Kaley Hamilton and the facts about his career, he could let Shelby in. Shelby's voice interrupted his thoughts.

"Um, Daniel, are you checking me out?"

Daniel looked down a bit sheepishly. "Damn. I thought I was doing a good job of keeping that on the DL."

"Not even close. You just spent several minutes staring at my legs."

Daniel laughed as he put his arm around her. "I'm sorry love, but it has to be said. You look good."

"Well, thank you very much Daniel. You don't look so bad yourself."

They made it to the rental car and put Shelby's bag in the trunk. Daniel looked over at her as they both got into the car.

"So, are you ready to hear the full truth, nothing but the truth so help me god, about why I asked you here?"

"Yes, please. I'm dying to know," Shelby said, breathless. She was curious what had caused Daniel to realize that she was right about Kaley (what did that even mean?!) and that she needed to be with him in Maui.

"Okay, first of all—am I like the only one who didn't know? Is Kaley really well known for this? The woman told me that I was coming to an intimate retreat with other publishers. Turns out, she's on vacation with two other couples who just happen to work in publishing! Can you believe that??"

"God, I knew it," Shelby said, leaning her head back. "And yes, she is well known for seducing and sleeping with her authors, although she does tend to sleep with the truly talented ones. So at least she knows how to pick them."

"I'm so sorry I reacted defensively when you shared your intuition with me. I was so sure it was my big break, that any other possibility seemed completely unimaginable. And I'm sorry that you seem to have to be the one to share all of these messages with me all of the time—messages that I really struggle to receive. My ego has had a hard time hearing a lot of this stuff. But, now, now I think I'm beginning to understand." Daniel reached out and grabbed her hand.

Shelby stared back into his eyes. Something more than Kaley Hamilton had happened over this past week. There was an even deeper reason why Daniel had asked her to come to Maui.

"So, you didn't invite me to be here solely to get Kaley Hamilton off of you?"

"Not even close. In fact, I hadn't even thought about it. I've been avoiding Kaley since the first night when I realized what was going on. I want to tell you everything, but first let's get out of this airport parking lot and get comfortable. It's too good of a story to not be told over a glass of wine."

―――――

Daniel had put together another incredible picnic for Shelby to welcome her to Maui. They drove from the airport straight to the beach, where Daniel promptly laid down a blanket and instructed Shelby to sit while he popped and poured some Hawaiian pineapple sparkling wine, along with an array of raw cheeses and crackers, fresh fruit, dark chocolate, and chicken skewers.

"There's a great little market not far from here that made this all possible. One of the gals there helped me decide what to get, so don't be too impressed. I had some serious help with this."

"Either way, it's really lovely. Thank you so much for putting it together."

Shelby took a long, deep breath as she sipped her wine and looked out over the ocean. The air smelled so sweet and the breeze was so soft and perfect—she couldn't believe she was in Maui. It was something out of a dream. She looked over at Daniel as he set out their food and smiled. She felt so sure he was her guy. She didn't know what that meant or how long she would have him for, but she knew that there was no other man she wanted to spend this time with than him.

Daniel caught her gaze. "What's up? You okay?" He came over and sat down on the blanket beside her.

"Everything is perfect. I was thinking how I wouldn't want to be anywhere else but here, with you."

She leaned in, kissing his lips softly, releasing ever so gently, letting her lips lightly dance along with his, taking her time and letting him feel her hot breath. He reached up, placing his hand along her jaw, tracing his fingers along her neck. Daniel felt so much energy moving throughout his body that he felt dizzy. He pulled back, looking at Shelby.

"Did you feel that?"

"The rush of energy that felt like we were going to topple over?"

"Um, yeah—that. Is that normal for you? Cause I've never felt anything like it before." Something about their connection was so intense it felt like they might burst right out of their bodies.

"No. That is definitely not normal for me," Shelby said, half playfully, half stoically. "But I've heard that the energy in Hawaii is less grounded, which allows spirits to connect more easily with the physical realms and for energy to be felt more intensely. So maybe that's why we're feeling it even more."

Her words hit Daniel like a ton of bricks. That explained why his mother had appeared before him for the first time in 11 years, in Hawaii. She hadn't even appeared in his dreams over the past 11 years—that he remembered anyway. But, he had never been to Hawaii either. And like his mother had shared, he was so enveloped in his grief that it was impossible for her to get through to him. But now, with Shelby in his life, he had become more open and definitely more confident. Being in Hawaii added a whole new element for him, as he claimed his work as an author—with or without an agent like Kaley Hamilton. It was the perfect timing for her to appear and give him her messages. And ever since she showed herself to him, he couldn't stop writing, the words were flowing out of him so effortlessly. He had to tell Shelby all of it. Now.

"Shelby?"

"Yes, Daniel."

"It's time for me to tell you why I asked you to come here."

Shelby's brow furrowed a bit. Had something bad happened? He hadn't hooked up with Kaley Hamilton from what she gathered from their conversation in the airport parking lot. Shelby couldn't imagine anything more dramatic and terrible than that.

"Is it bad?" Shelby whispered.

"Oh no, it's not bad," he said, and Shelby felt the muscles in her jaw relax, although she hadn't realized she was clenching them. He continued, "But, it is rather odd."

Shelby laughed, tossing her head back in relief. "Well, odd I can handle. Lay it on me. What happened that made you call me up demanding that I meet you on this island?" She was having fun with him now.

Daniel reached out and squeezed her hand. "You're probably going to scream 'I told you so!' at me. But anyway, here goes…" Shelby squeezed Daniel's hand back. She noticed his hand was quivering ever so slightly.

"My mom visited me in my room the other night."

Shelby gasped, covering her hand over her mouth. "You mean, like in a dream?" she asked in a muffled tone.

"No, not like in a dream."

"Like, in person?!" Shelby's voice was reaching a higher pitch as she tried her best to contain her excitement.

"Yes." Daniel replied.

"Holy shit!"

"You're telling me. I freaked out. Like massively freaked out. I couldn't even let her say what she needed to. I kept telling her to leave, and I burst into tears. I feel terrible that I couldn't handle having her in front of me like that."

Shelby reached out, running her hands through Daniels hair.

"Sweetie, it's not normal for human beings to see non-physical entities. It totally makes sense that you would feel fear…Were you able to get any part of the message from her?" Shelby was hesitant to ask this. She didn't want Daniel to feel worse about what had transpired. But, she was awfully curious what was so important that his mom had to show up in person to deliver the message. Besides, why wasn't she hounding Shelby with whatever the message was, like she had done before?

Because he's ready now. And the energy in Maui gave me the perfect portal to appear before him. Besides I couldn't give a message about you to you. That didn't work before.

Daniel's mother's voice floated into Shelby's awareness. It was the first time she heard from her in a long while—since the last message delivery imploded, that is.

And so, it *was* true that Hawaii's energy served as a portal for the non-physical to easily reveal itself, Shelby thought. Hearing it as a possibility and having it confirmed by a non-physical energy are two very different things. Shelby couldn't wait to share this new knowledge with Kathryn and Scott.

Daniel was relieved to be able to share this otherworldly experience with someone, especially someone like Shelby who had already had several experiences with the other side.

"She was able to get a message to me, thankfully. Even though I was so distraught after seeing her, I immediately laid back down and went into a deep sleep. And then, she came to me in a dream, and we were sitting and talking. And…"

Daniel didn't know how he was supposed to tell a woman he had only known a month that she was the woman he was meant to be with. Per the mandates of his dead mother. He was pretty sure he had lost his mind. Although it didn't feel like it at all. It felt more like he had finally located a part of himself that had been yearning to be discovered.

"Daniel, whatever it is, you can tell me. As long as you feel comfortable telling me that is. Don't push yourself. You've been through a lot in this past week."

Shelby was right—discovering that his "big break" was actually a ploy to seduce him (When did that ever happen? Daniel knew that at some point one of his novel's characters was going to go through something like this. It was too good of a story not to share!), and his mother had appeared in front of him, even though she had been dead for 11 years, to tell him that he was meant to be with the woman in front of him, and that he had important work to do. Oh, and that she was proud of him. Daniel's eyes welled up with tears as he recounted the feeling of his mother's arms wrapped around him and her words whispering in his ear. Words he had not heard in so long. He had tortured himself believing that he was a disappointment, that she would not be pleased with who he had become. But she had been. And she had been there watching the entire time.

Daniel looked up at Shelby, and a few tears fell from his face. Could his mother be right? Was she the woman he was meant to spend his life with? Before meeting Shelby, Daniel didn't know if he would ever truly feel love after losing his mother. Now that he knew he hadn't really lost her, that she was there loving him, looking after him all along, his whole life felt and looked differently. Was Shelby truly his lifelong love? Looking into her eyes, he heard a voice whisper, "Yes." Immediately he was covered in chills and goosebumps as energy raced into his crown. He closed his eyes and tears continued to fall.

When he opened his eyes, Shelby was there, her face filled

with love and support.

"She said...she said..." Shelby was sitting close to him on the blanket now. The waves of the ocean lapped softly nearby and a couple walked past them, hand-in-hand. The sun danced on their shoulders, and Daniel felt safe and serene. Whatever happened, everything would be okay. He had to stop fighting the flow and follow this, letting it lead him wherever he was meant to be.

"She said we're meant to be together and that she had been trying to communicate with me for years, but that you were the portal with which she could finally reach me. She said I have important work I'm meant to do in the world and that you are a part of that." Daniel let it all tumble out, trusting that Shelby could handle this revelation.

Shelby took a drink of her wine, swallowing forcefully. When she looked over at Daniel, tears filled her eyes.

"I don't know what to say Daniel. It's a hell of a message, that's for sure." Shelby took a deep breath, and leaned in to kiss Daniel. "You see," she continued. "I have known that since we first met. But, I was beginning to think I might be a little nuts for feeling that way."

Daniel pulled Shelby close to him, and she buried her face in his arms. Tears fell from both of their eyes. They kissed again, slowly, letting what Daniel had said sink into their consciousness.

"It *is* a hell of a message, isn't it?" Daniel quipped.

They both laughed, holding on to one another, as the sun began to descend around them. This was their life. And it was good.

―――――

Daniel wasn't sure what came over him, but as soon as he unlocked the door to his room, he picked Shelby up with one swoop his arms under both her legs, her arms wrapped loosely around his neck, and carried her in. She let out a yelp and began laughing hysterically. She was laughing so hard that Daniel had no choice but to follow her lead, setting her down gently on the bed and then falling onto it as well, enveloped in the warmth of love that was between them and the laughter that cascaded out of every cell in their bodies.

After several minutes of lying in their love and laughter, Shelby stopped, looking intently into Daniel's eyes. Instinctively, Daniel grabbed her, pulling her to him and covering her in kisses. Shelby arched her back, letting her blonde hair fall back while Daniel's lips trailed down her chest, over her sundress, down to her smooth, soft, tan legs and then back up again. He lay there on top of her, their breath synching up in ragged exhales, their foreheads pressed against one another.

"It's time," Shelby turned and whispered into his ear.

Daniel felt it too and knew that they had reached the moment they both had been waiting for—clarity about their love for one another. Sharing his mother's message was mildly terrifying to say out loud, but also freeing. They were free to love one another. Somehow, his mom, although on the other side, had done what was needed to bring them together. Now they were here, together, to unify their bodies with what their hearts and souls already knew.

Daniel didn't respond with words, instead he slowly pulled the straps of Shelby's sundress down over her arms, chest, and down around her waist. Shelby was not wearing a bra. Daniel caught his breath. He hadn't been expecting this, but the sight of her voluptuous breasts stirred in him a deep desire that he had not felt before with any other woman.

Shelby reached up and stroked his hair, her head tilted to one side, desire filling her eyes. Daniel sat up, taking off his shirt, unbuttoning it a bit clumsily, his breath becoming stronger still at the sight and touch of her. He lay back down, allowing his bare, chiseled chest to lie on top of Shelby's. A wave of heat passed through both of their bodies. Daniel felt energy circulating all around him. A light breeze wafted against his back.

"Oh. My. God. Do you feel that, Daniel?" Shelby said.

Feel it? He was so consumed by the fire between their two

chests, he could barely lie still.

"There's light and heat all around us Shelby."

"Yes," Shelby moaned.

Daniel pressed his mouth to Shelby's, letting it envelop hers, their tongues dancing in perfect harmony. Flitting, licking, tickling, their tongues and nipples pressed together creating a circuit of heat that was otherworldly. Daniel was gasping for breath, the sexual and spiritual energy between them overwhelming his ability to think.

Shelby reached down into Daniel's pants, feeling his hardness.

"Ohhhh," Daniel moaned, his eyes meeting Shelby's. "Your touch...is...unbelievable."

Daniel kissed Shelby even more intensely, drawing them both up into a seated position, hoisting Shelby over him, her legs straddling his.

"You are the most beautiful woman I have ever known," he said, as he stroked her hair back from her face.

Shelby's gaze softened, and Daniel could see the desire in her eyes brewing with love.

"Make love to me Daniel."

Shelby wrapped her arms and legs tightly around Daniel and began kissing him— gently at first, gradually letting the tension build as she used her tongue to tease him. She bit his lip ever so slightly, making him give out a slight moan.

"I want you Daniel."

Shelby moved to his ear, kissing softly around the edges, then using her tongue to seduce him, feeling his hardness pushing firmly into the flesh of her thigh. Daniel couldn't keep his hands in one place, he was desperate to feel every bit of Shelby. He let his hands caress her thighs, sinking his fingers into the flesh on her ass. As she licked his ear, Daniel gently bit her shoulder, working his way up to her neck. He wanted to devour every inch of her. And that was exactly what he was about to do.

Daniel hoisted Shelby up from her straddled position over him, practically standing on the bed. Carefully, he pulled down the rest of her dress, removing it completely and revealing her hot pink satin thong. Daniel's hands held Shelby's hips while he leaned in to kiss her panties, letting his hot breath cover her.

"Oh, Daniel," Shelby said as she stroked his head, tugging at his hair. She wanted him. Badly.

It was time for his clothes to be removed as well. Shelby lay down on the bed, and Daniel removed his pants, his charcoal gray boxer briefs sticking to him, the heat was so penetrating.

Daniel laid gently on top of Shelby, holding her, kissing her, pressing himself into her as he felt Shelby's legs spread wide, inviting him in. She was ready for him. They stared into one another's eyes, instinctively synching up their breath, feeling the excitement within both of their bodies, now feeling as one. Daniel could feel their chakras aligning, as the major energy centers located up their spines coalesced. The swirling energy around them emanated in and outside of their bodies, leaving him light-headed and aroused.

"Shelby, I want you." Daniel breathed.

"Yes, Daniel, yes."

Daniel reached across the bed to the nightstand, grabbing a condom. Shelby smiled, loving how well prepared he was. He had the sense to pick up a box while out putting their picnic together earlier that day, just in case things went the way he wanted them to. The way they were happening now.

"Here, let me do this for you," Shelby said as she switched places with him, climbing on top of him.

Shelby then leaned down, placing her lips on his erection, letting her tongue encircle him. Daniel moaned, only turning her on further, while his hands gripped her hair, pulling it firmly.

Shelby slowly lifted up, placing the condom carefully on Daniel. Their eyes locked as Shelby moved to sit on top of him. Daniel's hands firmly held her hips, and Shelby leaned down, kissing him lightly, their eyes remaining locked. Shelby nodded and Daniel did as well. They knew. They were now ready to merge together as one.

Shelby carefully guided Daniel inside of her, inch by inch as they breathed together in unison. As he entered her, he lost all grasp of words or thoughts, there was simply nothing left. Their energy pulsated inside of Shelby, while Daniel felt his energy exploding deep inside of her. Shelby began to rock her pelvis on top of him.

"There is light all around you, Shelby," Daniel whispered. He couldn't help but notice an effervescent glow around her entire body, even in the dimly lit room.

Shelby's head tilted back as she moaned, her hands pressed against Daniel's strong chest.

"I can feel you in every cell of my body Daniel."

Shelby rocked her pelvis with greater speed, letting Daniel follow her lead, although his breath was ragged, unable to sustain their mutual rhythm. He felt as though he might burst—the sight of her, the feel of her, and the energy of it all. Shelby watched him closely, recognizing that having him inside of her seemed to give her direct access to his thoughts.

"I can feel you Daniel. You're close."

Daniel nodded, swallowing hard.

Shelby intuitively slowed her pace, taking her time and Daniel, his head tilted back, was unable to take much more of it, the intensity was bursting throughout his entire body.

"Daniel, Daniel," Shelby began chanting his name, quickening her pace.

Daniel was so overtaken by the heat radiating from Shelby's body. He felt all of his senses expand—he could see, feel, taste, and hear the energy move up, in and throughout her body.

"Oh, my god, Daniel. Oh my god." Shelby was jerking now, riding him harder and faster than before, leaning back to support herself by holding his thighs. Daniel's hands were locked firmly onto her waist, watching as she led them both to climax.

"Shelby, I'm there."

Shelby looked down at Daniel, desire fierce in her eyes, bucking him. He could feel her heat ready to explode. Their eyes locked.

"Daniel. Daniel, Daniel!"

Shelby began screaming his name as waves of pleasure released from her body, Daniel followed suit, screaming Shelby's name, jolting upright from the power of their orgasms. They both clung to each other, as the rocking began to slow and the waves of pleasure continued on.

"I love you Shelby." Daniel said softly, his face pressed against her shoulder.

"I love you Daniel," Shelby whispered back.

8

Shelby awoke the next morning to the distant yet soft lullaby of the ocean and the smell of coffee. Slowly sitting up, Shelby sleepily pulled off her eye mask only to be faced with a half-naked Daniel, donning navy blue boxer briefs, making coffee while humming a tune she didn't recognize. Even from behind, Shelby found Daniel to be the sexiest man she had ever seen. His strong, buttery tan back and legs seemed to glow in the sunlight, making Shelby feel dizzy. She lay back down with a small sigh, reliving last night's events.

After they made love, they lay in bed for another hour or so naked, Shelby lying in Daniel's arms while he stroked her hair. They talked about the energy created from their sexual union and its power. Neither of them had ever experienced anything like it before. It was truly otherworldly, for both of them. Daniel was also able to share more with Shelby about how his writing had been transformed by their coming together and by his mother's recent in-person visit. Both he and Shelby were in awe that a novel unlike anything he had ever written before was being birthed and spurred on by all of the magic they were experiencing. Shelby was able to tell Daniel about the visit with the psychic at the Saturday Market, as well. He was flabbergasted by the accuracy and impact of the words the woman spoke.

"Why didn't you tell me? I would have totally been down with you sharing that guidance." Daniel exclaimed.

"Yeah, I'm going to invite myself on your trip? There's no way I could have done that. It needed to come from you." Shelby responded.

He could see her point, but encouraged her to share whatever guidance came in. "There's no need for us to have any more secrets about this stuff. I know I had a hard time initially, but I get it now. I know it's one of the many gifts that women possess and that men can benefit from. And I want to hear about whatever intuitive guidance comes in, that you feel comfortable sharing, of course."

This made Shelby feel so completely safe and comfortable, knowing that she could share freely with him. Recalling this conversation, brought those feelings of comfort and warmth back to her. Then, suddenly she remembered that they had said "I love you" last night after making love. And as they drifted off to sleep, Daniel had said again, "I really do love you Shelby."

Shelby had never said "I love you" so early on in a relationship, let alone immediately following sex. Wasn't that merely the hormones talking anyway? Shelby noticed that she felt slightly insecure about it. What would today bring? Would the "L" word make an appearance again? And what were they up to after all? Messages from his deceased mother, sex that felt more like a spiritual experience than physical, an impromptu meet-up across the Pacific—what in the world were they doing?

Whatever it was, it felt delicious, and Shelby couldn't help but exhale a sigh of love and joy. Daniel heard her and turned around, beaming back at her smiling face.

"Good morning, beautiful," Daniel said as he came over, kissing Shelby tenderly on the lips. "How did you sleep?"

"I was out. I don't think I've slept that deeply in years."

"I know, right? It's something about the island energy. The stewardess on my flight warned me, she said things happen differently when you're on the islands—and I've got to say, I'm a believer now."

"Well, I've only been here one night, but if it's any indication," Shelby said with a wink, "I'd say I'm a believer, too."

"Last night was incredible, wasn't it?" Daniel sat down on the bed next to Shelby, holding her hand.

"There are no words," Shelby said, reaching out and caressing his face.

"Come on, I want to do something with you. Come here," he said as he guided her out of bed, holding onto her hand.

"What, what is it?"

"I want to dance with you."

"Where? Here? Right now?"

"Yes, right here, right now, at the foot of the bed, in between the dresser and mirror and the mini-kitchenette. Are you game?"

Shelby wasn't much of a dancer and felt self-conscious. Besides, she wasn't sure how many moves she could bust in her mid-thigh-level pink polka dotted, razorback chemise. "And what music will we be dancing to Mr. Tillman?"

"The music from the ocean," Daniel said, as he placed his other arm around her waist and began dancing with her, their feet shuffling in sync. Daniel pressed his face to Shelby's, humming a soft tune of something he didn't know, but yet somehow felt familiar.

Shelby's unease quickly dissipated as they found their flow, dancing slowly in the room, the sun streaming in, the ocean sounds in the background, and the knowing that they were exactly where they were meant to be. Shelby was certain it was one of the single most romantic moments in her life.

Just then, someone knocked on the door. "Daniel? Daniel, are you there?"

It was Kaley Hamilton.

Daniel had managed to make excuses each morning when Kaley came by and he figured she was getting the hint. Apparently not. He hadn't thought about how he would introduce Kaley and Shelby, and how awkward that might be for Shelby—and for him.

Shelby looked up at him, her eyes wide. She mouthed the words, "Kaley Hamilton?!" Daniel could tell by the look in her eyes that she was not pleased. Besides, they were both half naked.

Daniel had two choices: he could answer the door and get the awkwardness over with or drag it out a little bit longer. Shelby mouthed, "Not now," shaking her head vigorously.

"Um, Kaley," Daniel called out, and Shelby ran into the bathroom. "I just got out of the shower. What do you need?"

There was a long pause and Daniel thought perhaps she had left. But, he wasn't that lucky.

"Oh good, we are getting ready to go down to Lahaina for some shopping. We would love for you to join us," Kaley called out. "And um, we're going to be talking about next year's top book selections," she sang out, half under her breath, but loud enough for Daniel to hear.

"Sorry Kaley, I've got other plans. But have a great time."

More silence.

"Well I hope we get to see you before this trip is over. Jonathan mentioned that he would really like to take a look at your work."

Daniel rolled his eyes. Jonathan probably had zero intention of looking at any words Daniel had written—like, ever. He wasn't about to fall for that again.

"Okay, sounds good. Have fun Kaley." Daniel heard the click-clack of Kaley's heels and breathed a sigh of relief. He turned and saw Shelby peeking out. She mouthed, "Is she gone?"

"Yes, sweetie, you can speak in a normal voice now."

"What was she doing coming by your room…it's—," Shelby picked up the digital clock by the bed. "It's only 9 a.m."

Daniel rubbed his hands on his temples, looking down. "She comes by every morning. It's just annoying now. You'd think she would get the hint."

"Maybe it's time to tell her you're not interested directly,"

Shelby suggested, trying to keep the irritation out of her voice.

Daniel could feel her tension, and didn't want Shelby to worry. Kaley was not the kind of woman he would ever want to be with. Not to mention that his mother had worked very hard to let him know that Shelby was the woman he was meant to share his life with, and he wasn't about to blow it.

Daniel walked over to Shelby, placing both hands on her shoulders.

"Shelby, there is no other woman that I would ever want to be with. Let alone Kaley Hamilton. I really want you to know this and feel it from deep within me," Daniel placed one hand on his heart. "Can you trust that I am being honest with you?"

The truth was Shelby did feel it from him. Her mind kept trying to fit the scenario into old stories where she had been lied to before or from high school when her freshman boyfriend had cheated on with a senior cheerleader. But, deep within her, she knew that no matter what the scenario, Daniel simply wasn't the kind of man who would behave that way.

"I know, and I *can* feel it from you. It just creeps me out a little bit."

Daniel laughed, "You're creeped out? I am beyond creeped out from all of this. I thought I was coming here for my big break."

Shelby leaned into Daniel, wrapping her arms around his neck. "You've had it rough here Mister. All this tropical paradise and hot sex and everything."

Daniel smacked her behind, and squeezed her tight. "Well, you do have a point. I was clearly meant to come to the islands."

As Daniel uttered those words, their truth rang even more clearly to both of them, at the same time. Shelby couldn't believe that they hadn't seen it before. "Oh whoa. Kaley really is an angel, because she got you to come here. And that was the key to your mom being able to appear before you, give you the message, and fly me over here, so we could discover all of this," Shelby's hands circled around as she tried to gesture what all of "this" was.

"Yes! I can see it now, too. Damn. You're good," Daniel kissed her, letting his tongue stroke her mouth softly. He pulled back and said, "And I assume the 'this' you're referencing is love. Am I right?"

Before she could answer, Daniel planted another kiss on her already moist lips.

The next five days were bliss for Daniel and Shelby. Daniel spent the mornings writing up a storm, while Shelby slept in and then went for a jog on the beach. By the time she returned, they were ready to spend the day making love and exploring Maui.

First it was massages and soaking pools at The Grand Wailea. Shelby didn't think she could leave the aromatic hydrotherapy baths or the cascading waterfall massage, even if it meant reconnecting with Daniel for the rest of the day. It was so heavenly she almost didn't notice that everyone was naked. She had shown up with her bathing suit on after the massage. The woman working in the redwood sauna took one look at her, smiled and said, "Sweetie, you're not going to need that." She put her hand out and Shelby, taken aback and a bit out of it from her massage, stripped down and handed over her bathing suit. But, the woman was right. She didn't need her suit, and she walked out of the spa feeling like a million bucks. Well, from that and the delicious lovemaking with Daniel that morning.

Daniel had never known his life to flow so effortlessly. The writing was pouring out of him. The combined impact of meeting Shelby and the visit from his mother had opened something up within him that had been closed for as long as he could remember. As he walked out of The Grand Wailea's "his" spa area to meet up with Shelby, he had a moment where he could see outside of himself. It was like he had left his body and was observing himself walking down the hall anticipating Shelby's arrival.

His life felt like a dream. Here he was in paradise, with the woman he was going to spend his life with, and felt so confident about his writing career that he didn't even notice that nothing had really changed—he didn't have a book deal and hadn't been discovered. But, his writing was flowing like never before and although he didn't know what might happen, he knew something big was on its way. All he had to do was keep writing. Daniel stopped, leaning against a wall to steady himself. All that steam and heat must have really gotten to him. Just then, he saw Shelby come out of the ladies' spa area, walking toward him. She was absolutely glowing in a spaghetti strap lavender tank and white shorts with flip-flops, her blonde hair pulled up high in a ponytail on top of her head.

"Daniel, are you okay?" Shelby could tell right away something was "off."

"Honestly Shelb, I feel like I'm having an out-of-body experience. As I was walking down the hallway, I had a moment where I was observing myself walking and seeing how incredible my life was. It tripped me out."

Shelby wrapped her arms around Daniel, holding him close.

"Dead people sending us messages, then showing up for in-person chats, and now out-of-body experiences. That sounds about right for us," Shelby quipped.

Daniel began laughing and the laughter helped to ground him.

"Apparently, this is the way our relationship is going," Daniel pulled Shelby back to face him, kissing her gently. "But, I wouldn't have it any other way. Now, let's go walk on the beach."

―――

By the time Daniel and Shelby came back from walking on the beach, it was early evening. As they came up the pathway, Daniel cringed as he saw Kaley Hamilton and friends sitting outside, drinking chilled white wine and barbecuing. He stopped, pausing to decide what to do, holding Shelby's hand and shielding her behind him.

It was too late though.

"Daniel! So lovely to see you. We've been missing you. Come join us," Kaley called over.

"Damnit," Daniel muttered under his breath. "Well Shelb, are you ready to meet the infamous Kaley Hamilton? It looks as though the time has come."

Shelby was still riding the high from the lovemaking-spa-beach day and couldn't have cared less about Kaley Hamilton.

"Bring it on," she said, through a smile.

As they approached the gathering, Kaley came right over to them decked out in a fuchsia wrap dress and long, dangly diamond earrings with fuchsia colored jewels. She immediately gave Shelby the up and down, and then turned to address Daniel.

"And who is this Daniel? I didn't know you had a friend here in Maui," Kaley cooed.

"This is actually my girlfriend, she lives in Portland as well, and her name is Shelby. Shelby, this is Kaley Hamilton— "

"The illustrious literary agent, oh yes, I am quite familiar," Shelby interjected reaching out her hand to shake Kaley's.

Kaley raised one eyebrow, shaking Shelby's hand as well.

"Well, I had no idea you had a girlfriend Daniel."

"That's because our relationship is strictly professional, Kaley," Daniel replied. He heard Jonathan chuckle and give a nod to Richard— both of whom were seated a foot or so away.

"Hey Daniel," Jonathan called out. "Why don't you and your lady join us for a cocktail? Richard was just getting ready to pull out the big guns and make us some margaritas."

Daniel looked over at Shelby. She nodded and he squeezed her hand. They casually walked past Kaley and over to where Richard and Jonathan sat.

"Sounds great guys, let's do this."

Kaley Hamilton glared in their direction and headed back to her condo.

―――

An hour later, Shelby and Daniel were engaged in a riveting

conversation with Jonathan, while the others were seated at the picnic table snacking and chatting. Kaley rejoined the group (apparently she had only gone back to her condo to get a light silver pashmina), and while she looked casually over in their direction a few times, she seemed to be less focused on Daniel since Shelby's arrival. This left room for Daniel to connect more with Jonathan in an authentic way. As it turned out, Jonathan was wildly passionate about the Law of Attraction and they were all discussing how to work with the law in daily life.

"I'm telling you, I believe this law is for real, but when I receive shitty service at a restaurant, or someone cuts me off in traffic, I get really frustrated. I know that the Universe is showing me, "me," on some level—especially if it triggers me—but you know sometimes I wish the Universe would give me a break. Can't I be in a crappy mood and not have it come right back to me?" Jonathan asked.

Daniel and Shelby laughed. Although Jonathan's comment caused Daniel to pause briefly to reflect on Kaley's behavior. If the Universe was always showing him, "him," what was Kaley showing him? Where in his life was he not being 100 percent truthful? Where was he pretending he wanted one thing, but really wanted another? He was going to have to do some further reflecting on it. Nothing was random, he knew that, so there was some investigating that needed to take place.

Shelby chimed in, "Oh, Jonathan, I know all about that. My boss is a complete ass. He never gets back to me in a timely fashion, he hands out orders, and he never checks in with others before making important decisions. I can't figure out how I attracted him into my life…" Shelby took a long pause.

"Something coming to mind?" Jonathan inquired.

"Actually, yes. Talking about this out loud is bringing something up. I acted a bit like that with my younger sisters growing up. I was bossy and didn't listen to them—and thought I was always right. And actually, even though it's not exactly the same manifestation, I still carry some of that within me when it comes to my sisters. I don't boss them like I used to, but I still think I am right. Shit. I think I'm starting to realize how my boss was able to come into my experience. He's showing me that part of myself that still needs to be healed!"

"Nice work, Shelb!" Daniel said, fist-bumping her. They both cracked up. Fist-bumping was so ridiculous, it always made them laugh.

"So, now," Jonathan said, leaning in. "Now, you get to the fun part. Just by observing this inside of you, it will begin to shift. You'll notice more when you act that way with your sisters and you'll be able to adjust. And then, you get to choose what healing method you want to use to release that old story and vibration. Do you have good healers you can lean on?"

"Hmm…good question. Daniel has raved about BodyTalk and I have an intuitive healer I see every six months or so. Maybe I should schedule a session to clear out this old vibration."

"I highly recommend it," Jonathan said. "It definitely allows you to more quickly shed that old story and then manifest more of what you do want. Like maybe a nicer boss."

"Or no boss at all," Shelby laughed as she looked over at Daniel.

Just then, Jonathan's wife, Emily, came over. "I thought I heard you guys talking about the Law of Attraction. You do not want to get Jonathan started. He can talk endlessly about this topic," she said laughing.

"Too late!" Daniel and Shelby said in unison, bursting into laughter.

"I don't know why I was hanging out over there," Emily said, "The party is obviously here. Daniel, how do you know Kaley again?"

"Well, I don't actually," said Daniel. "We met at the Willamette Writers Conference, the same day I met Shelby. I met Shelby right before my scheduled pitch with Kaley and our conversation completely relaxed and invigorated me. By the time I went in to meet Kaley, I no longer felt nervous. Somehow that worked for me and she was interested. Then, the next thing I knew, she invited me to Maui to "network," Daniel used air quotes, "with others in the industry. But once I got here, I got the impression that you all weren't exactly here to talk business."

Jonathan and Emily exchanged looks, looks that only couples who had been together for some time could exchange. Jonathan chuckled and then said, "Kaley means well, but sometimes she gets a little ahead of herself." He reached into his back pocket, pulling out a gold-embossed business card. "But honestly, Daniel, I really like your energy and passion. Send me your manuscript and I'll see if it has potential at our publishing house. If not, I can definitely make a recommendation on where it may be a fit."

Daniel smiled, glancing over at Shelby. "Jonathan, thank you. I will definitely send you my manuscript and if it's a fit, great—if not, that's okay too. But I appreciate the opportunity all the same."

"It's a sign, either way, right?" Jonathan said.

"Absolutely." The two men raised their glasses in unison.

It was in that moment that the trip to Maui came into even clearer perspective for both Daniel and Shelby.

"I'm going to miss you," Shelby said as she packed her suitcase.

Daniel came up behind her, wrapping his arms around her and nuzzling into her ear. "I'm going to miss you, too," he said, squeezing her tightly.

Unfortunately, he hadn't been able to get them out of Maui on the same flight on the same day, so now they would be journeying back on separate Hawaiian Air flights. Shelby later that afternoon and he late the next day. They hadn't discussed how things might change in Portland. Daniel had briefly given thought to what he would do with his studio since his lease was expiring soon. And now that being a writer was no longer something he had to painstakingly try to make happen he no longer needed a bachelor pad writing studio. He had a solid outline and start on his second novel in Maui, and felt inspired to self-publish *Shannon Town* regardless of whether Jonathan found a home for it at his publishing house.

Life was opening up for him in ways he hadn't seen coming and Kaley, Maui, Shelby, Jonathan, and his mom were all important pieces of the puzzle that had led him to this place. He knew he was ready to expand and as far as he was concerned going back to life as it was prior to Shelby was no longer an option. And while he had never lived with a woman before, it did occur to him that perhaps that was next for him and Shelby. As much as he was going to miss her over the next 24 hours, he also knew it was a good opportunity for him to connect with his deeper wisdom to get clearer about what the future held.

Shelby leaned her head back into Daniel and sighed. "I think I'm all set to go. Will you drive me?"

Daniel turned her around, "Of course I will. I am determined to get every last possible second with you that I can."

She smiled, standing on her tip toes kiss Daniel.

"And how will you spend the next 24 hours Mr. Tillman?"

"Oh well, that's a big secret. But it does involve sitting on the beach and thinking about you. And possibly some additional 'thinking,' about you in the evening and in the morning."

Shelby giggled. "Tease. Although I'll probably be in the same boat. Flying, reading Paulo Coelho, and 'thinking' about you. Yep, sounds about right."

As they walked out to Daniel's car, Shelby's bag in tow, they both looked up at the clear blue sky, smiling.

"Who knew all this was in store for us when you arrived last week, eh?"

"Well, your mom kind of did."

"Touché," said Daniel, grabbing Shelby and kissing her deeply. The Universe had seen this coming all along. He couldn't help but wonder how things might have been different over the past 11 years if he had known that his mom was with him the whole time.

―――

Looking out the airplane window, Shelby couldn't help but feel a mixture of sadness, joy, love, and hope. She had no idea what was next for her and Daniel, but she could feel that big changes were on the way. Being with Daniel provided her with so much inspiration that she was unbelievably clear that working as an assistant at *Hello Portland* was no longer serving her highest good. She needed to be creating, and jewelry was her passion. She had woken up early one morning in Maui, filled with inspiration to form a partnership with a local women's shelter and have a small portion of sales go to support the women. Having been raised in an abusive home, Shelby knew all too well the devastation that was possible. Being able to support women who, like her mom, desperately needed outside help, filled her with hope and joy.

Now, she had to figure out how to make it all happen. She had some money in savings, but nowhere near the suggested nine months of expenses that all financial gurus claim one must have before stepping into their own business. Shelby knew there had to be a way to bring her dream into reality. The pull inside of her was strong, and it was saying that it was time to step into living her passion. Having Daniel in her life was one part of this, and now she felt she wouldn't be complete until all of her was living in a state of passion. She hadn't discussed this with Daniel, as there were too many other delicious activities taking place, but as the plane took off and Maui faded into the distance, Shelby knew returning to Portland would mean embarking on a more expanded life journey.

Although her relationship with Daniel was super-new, Shelby couldn't help but wonder if perhaps living together might be part of that expansion. She instantly felt compelled to dial up Kathryn to get her perspective. Flying nixed that. And Kathryn was probably neck-deep in the commitment ceremony planning process, Shelby mused.

She and Scott were holding a ceremony in a few weeks on November 11. And while it had originally started out as a simple affair, it had quickly grown into quite the event. Shelby had heard that 111 people would be attending the partially indoor and outdoor event at McMenamins Grand Lodge. Kathryn had asked Shelby to stand up with her, along with her friend Jess and sister Audrey. Their friendship had immediately felt like a deep spiritual, sisterly bond that both she and Kathryn valued. Shelby was touched that she was included in Kathryn's commitment ceremony, even though they had only been friends for a little less than a year.

"Excuse me miss," Shelby's thoughts were interrupted by the woman sitting next to her. "Sorry to bother you, but I couldn't help but notice the book you're reading. Is it by Paulo Coelho?" the woman asked.

"Yes! This is one of my favorites, I'm reading it over again," Shelby said as she picked up *Eleven Minutes*, turning it over and then smoothing the cover. Kathryn had turned her on to Paulo's inspiring work. "Are you a Coelho fan?"

The woman, slightly demure, with light ash blonde hair, glasses, and wearing a long jean skirt and floral button-up blouse, nodded eagerly. "I am. I feel so connected when I read his work."

"I know, me too! And this one is so sexy. I've recently fallen in love and it's been fun reading this book while it's all happening."

"Oh, congrats. Your whole face lit up when you mentioned falling in love. Is this guy the one you want to spend your life with?"

Shelby paused. Did she even believe in spending her life with one person? Her parents' estranged marriage that ended in divorce always made Shelby leery of marriage, even though she always figured it would happen "someday." But now faced with a serious prospect in Daniel she had to re-evaluate. And if she did believe in one person for a lifetime, would it be Daniel? She knew she was meant to be in his life and he in hers. She knew without a shadow of a doubt that they had a deep and meaningful connection. She even thought of them living together. But forever? This would definitely be a Kathryn conversation.

In the meantime, she simply said, "Maybe," smiled weakly at the woman and turned her head to once again look out the airplane window.

―――――

Daniel sipped a glass of lemonade while staring out into the ocean from the courtyard of the condo property. He had dropped Shelby off an hour ago and immediately felt a slight emptiness with her gone. Kaley and the others had flown over to Kauai for an extended excursion, so Daniel had some time to reflect on his experience over the past 11 days.

"Mom," Daniel said quietly. He felt like he needed to connect with her, and while he wasn't sure if simply calling her name would do the trick, he figured it was worth a try.

Wind rustled the palm trees around him and he felt cold chills cover his torso and down his spine. "Mom is that you?" The breeze blew through again, this time with more of a gust. "Okay, I'm going to take that as a yes."

Daniel continued, "I think you're right. I think Shelby is the one for me. But I don't know how to do this—I've never even lived with a woman. I spent so much time protecting and cutting myself off from women after I lost you that I'm clueless now. I didn't feel worthy of giving and receiving deep love from a woman. I'm going to need a lot of help and guidance with this."

As he said this, the face of an intuitive BodyTalk healer that Daniel had seen before popped into his mind. He hadn't thought of her in months, but Gabby was quite gifted and had been a big part of the reason why Daniel made the leap to getting his studio and focusing solely on his writing.

"Are you telling me to schedule a session with Gabby for help with this big transition I'm in?" Daniel couldn't believe how quickly the image had popped into his mind and how sure he felt that his mom—right here in broad daylight, in the middle of a condominium property—was communicating with him.

The wind came through again, covering Daniel's entire body with chills.

"Okay, got it. I have a resource to help me with next steps. Thank you, mom. You are seriously the best. I only wish I had realized I could have been communicating with you for the past 11 years. Better late than never though, right?"

Daniel quickly felt the breeze again, only this time it seemed to circle him, as though his mother was wrapping her arms around his body, hugging him.

―――

Shelby wasn't home more than a half hour when her doorbell rang. After five hours on a plane, she was less than thrilled. The only thing she wanted to do was meditate, take a sea salt bath, and go to bed. But, that, apparently was not in the cards.

"Kathryn? What are you doing here? You didn't even call!" Shelby said as she opened the door to find Kathryn standing in front of her, a bottle of sparkling white in one hand and bridal magazines in the other.

"I figured that what you needed after five days with a man you clearly love…" Kathryn pointed her finger at Shelby as she walked in the door, "And don't even bother arguing with me, I could feel the love energy emanating all the way from Maui. What you needed was some good girl time with me and *Bride* magazine," Kathryn flopped down on the couch, dressed in her typical getup—workout gear of black leggings, a sports bra (today was purple), a white v-neck, three-quarter sleeve T-shirt and a purple (Kathryn was a huge fan of the color) sweatshirt.

"What, did you just get back from the gym? And now wine and bride stuff?" Shelby was having trouble hiding her irritation.

"Um, yeah, post-workout meal. I figured you would have some Maui chocolate and macadamias to go with this feast for rockstars. And don't give me attitude; you know you're dying to discuss how you're doing your hair at my commitment ceremony, along with how excited you are to bring Daniel as your date."

Shelby couldn't help but crack a smile. She *had* picked up some macadamia nuts and chocolate for Kathryn, and while she hadn't officially asked Daniel to the commitment ceremony, she planned to. And she really was dying to talk to Kathryn about her revelation that he felt like the guy for her, but that she didn't even know what to do with that realization.

Grabbing the bag of chocolate nuts, along with two glasses, she joined Kathryn on the couch.

"Okay, you got me. But less about my hair and more about the fact that I'm totally head over heels for this guy. I want to move in with him and spend my life staring into his gorgeous blue eyes. What is wrong with me?" Shelby moaned as she instinctively opened the bag of chocolates, taking a handful and giving the bag to Kathryn.

"Now, that's more like it Shelby!" she said playfully rubbing the top of Shelby's head, mussing her hair. "You're getting to the good stuff now. Trust me, I know about the love-induced freak-out. I had a big moment with Scott where I was like, "I can't do this!" And found myself ogling some stupid waiter. When you meet the guy, it can bring up all sorts of stuff. But, that's okay. You'll work through it."

"And how exactly do you suggest I do that? I almost found myself saying, 'Hey, since your lease is coming up on your studio and I'm ready to quit my job to go for my dream, let's merge our happy little solopreneur lives together.' On the airplane ride home, I realized I was in big trouble. Sure, I always thought I would end up with one person for the rest of my life at some point, but it suddenly seems like that rest of my life person is coming to me fast. But, Daniel is too fantastic of a man for me *not* to consider a future with him."

Kathryn sank back into the couch. "I get it girl. But know this, there *is* one man in this world that will make you want to believe in spending the rest of your life with one person. Besides, you can't think of it like that—it's too overwhelming. It's choosing him every day."

"How do you know you're going to choose Scott every day? Because having a commitment ceremony, getting married, whatever it is that you're doing, is saying, 'Hey everyone—look at the person I'm going to spend forever with!'"

"Okay, first of all smarty pants," Kathryn said as she poured them both a glass of wine. "We're having a commitment ceremony, because we feel that the institution of marriage has too much negativity attached to it. It's not the kind of energy that we want hanging over us or in our relationship dynamic. There's all this charge around divorce, and the roles of 'husband' and 'wife.' We understand that when we come together in a relationship, our souls have a contract. It may last a lifetime and it may not. But either way, relationship is a sacred contract that we want to honor. So, instead, we're creating a ritual of our own to commemorate our commitment to one another. Commitment is energetically a very powerful statement to make to yourself, one another, and the people you love most in the world—not to mention the Universe. And with a commitment ceremony, we are free to create it in the way we want, so that we don't fall prey to carrying out the roles we saw our parents or other loved ones emulate. We can create a partnership that truly honors each other as individuals and as a couple."

Shelby held her hand up in mock defense. "You don't have to explain it to me, but since you did, it sounds lovely. I just never know how to explain it to people. Anyway, please continue, as I know you have much more to say on this topic…"

Kathryn grinned. "Damn right I do," she held her glass up for a toast. "And as far as how do I know I'm going to choose Scott every day? It's simple—I don't." Kathryn took a sip of wine. "But, what I do know is that I'm going to wake up every morning and set the intention to be the most loving, giving, kick-ass person I know. And I know that if I'm being that full expression of myself, that Scott is the only man for me. So, no matter how irritated I get or whatever is coming up for me, he's the one I'm meant to do it with. I can feel it deep in my soul. And that, missy," Kathryn was pointing at Shelby again, "is worth a million commitment ceremonies."

Kathryn's eyes had grown misty and Shelby could feel the truth in her words. No matter what, Kathryn knew that Scott was her choice, the one she was meant to walk today's path with—and whatever the future held, they would both honor it with the sacredness that they were entering into their lives together with. Shelby took a sip of her wine as she felt her heart expand, knowing Daniel was the same for her as well.

9

Daniel's studio felt oddly different when he returned. As he tossed his keys on his desk, he had a strange feeling like his home no longer belonged to him, but to someone else.

He tried to get comfortable, but nothing seemed to work. He tried lying down, but sleep wouldn't come, even after his long flight. Instead he felt antsy and restless, as though he needed to be doing something else. He sat up and tried to meditate, but again, his mind went elsewhere—writing novels and thinking about Shelby. They had texted briefly when he landed, he let her know he had arrived and planned to rest, and then would call her. Nothing more.

As he sat on his bed, pillows propping him up as he leaned against the wall, legs crossed, palms face up, and eyes closed, he replayed some of their magical time together in Maui. He was forever changed by the two weeks. Now, what? His connection with Shelby felt stronger than merely a girlfriend. He felt an undeniable urge to merge his life with hers. Could they move in together? He had never lived with a woman before, but if he was going to do it, he knew Shelby had to be the one to do it with. Even so, taking that kind of step made Daniel nervous. He was in uncharted territory.

He looked back at his last text from Shelby.

Don't worry – do what u need 2 & let's chat when ur feeling up 2 it. So glad ur back! And so ready to b in ur arms. Xoxo

Shelby was like an angel to Daniel. An angel that he may have missed had his mother not come through from the other side to guide him. But, now what? Could he just jump into living together with her? Did that mean he wanted to marry her? He had to write. Sitting in "meditation" wasn't doing him an ounce of good, as his mind spun round and round. He hopped off the bed and meandered over to his desk and his computer.

Daniel closed his eyes and placed his hands over the keyboard, just as he had done the week before the Willamette Writers Conference and just as he had done in Maui. Somehow, his fingers knew exactly the story that needed to come out. A few pages in (he was around Chapter 8 of 11 in his new novel), Daniel began noticing that his character Phillip was at a crossroads that wasn't too unlike what he was experiencing in his own life. Sure, it was the late 1800s, but a man still battled with the pull to do his work and create a family. Daniel's character had a heart. He loved Jasmine, but also felt called to the open road.

Was Daniel feeling the same thing? Was there more that he was feeling called to beyond Shelby? His mind was so enmeshed in possibilities that he had to keep writing—there was nothing else for him to do. He had to let whatever the answer was for Phillip (and possibly him) come through. This was not something he could figure out with his mind. Two hours later, his fingers stopped moving and Daniel felt complete. Phillip now knew what he was going to do and the choice he had to make, and so did Daniel.

With that, he picked up the phone and called Shelby.

―――

"I love you."

Shelby had barely said "hello" when Daniel immediately interrupted her. He said it again in case she didn't catch it the first time.

"I love you."

"Well, hello there. I love you too. You doing okay?"

"Shelby, I am fantastic. I spent two hours working on my novel. The characters are winding down, they're making their choices and it's great. Really great. When can I see you?"

Shelby laughed.

"You're cute."

"Thank you. So, do you want to come by my place, say, in about an hour?"

"I would love to, however, I am otherwise predisposed. I'm not sure if I mentioned it to you or not, but my closest friends, Kathryn and Scott, are having a commitment ceremony next weekend and so I am helping the not-bride bride tonight with the other not-bridesmaids bridesmaids for last-minute preparations and such."

"Oh wow, that's so sweet of you. You're going to be at it all night?"

"Let me say this, we've got two bottles of red, some dark chocolate, and place cards, so yeah—it's gonna be a long night.
"

"Do you need any boy help?"

Shelby laughed again. "You are seriously. The cutest. Ever."

"I know. And thank you."

"Well...there is one thing I do need."

"Anything," Daniel wasn't sure what he was opening himself up to, but something about connecting with Shelby's energy made him come alive.

"I do need a date to the not-wedding wedding next Saturday. Are you available for that? Say around 4-ish?"

"I thought you were going to ask me to do some difficult man stuff like fix a carburetor or something. Date with a beautiful woman to a love-centered event? Done and done. I'm there. Just tell me what to wear and I'm yours."

"Perfect! This not-wedding wedding is totally casual; you could get away with khakis and a button-up. I will be standing up with the not-bride bride, so I'll be decked out in head-to-toe pink. Save your cheering for later. Hopefully, you won't mind being with the girl who looks like a bottle of Pepto-Bismol," Shelby laughed. She wasn't sure when she was ever so giggly with a man. But, something about the energy between her and Daniel made her giddy.

"I actually like Pepto-Bismol, so you're all set. And please let me know if there is anything else I can do to help out, okay?"

"Absolutely. And Daniel?"

"Yes, Shelby?"

"I love you."

Kathryn and Scott's big day arrived quickly. Fortunately, Shelby wasn't entirely wrapped up with not-wedding wedding duties all week and managed to sneak in a dinner with Daniel the night before. They played it low-key, choosing to spend time after dinner cuddled up on his navy blue couch, rubbing each other's feet, which eventually turned into full body massages. Shelby couldn't help but think about exactly this (particularly when Daniel was lightly kissing and caressing her back as she lay face down on his bed, softly moaning from the pleasure of it all) as she walked down the aisle with William, Scott's not-groomsman groomsman.

"You okay, Shelby?" William whispered out of the side of his mouth.

"Yeah, I'm fine, why?" Shelby whispered back.

"You're walking kind of fast, so wasn't sure where your head was at."

Shelby took a deep breath and slowed her pace. *Focus, Shelb*, she scolded herself.

Kathryn and Scott's commitment ceremony was a simple affair, but elegant and lovely all the same—much like Kathryn and Scott.

Fortunately, the Universe had blessed them with a sunny and clear, yet crisp November 11 day, so they were able to hold the ceremony outside. White chairs lined the lawn at Delia's Garden and a white trestle accented the stage area where Scott and Kathryn would profess their love to one another. As Shelby walked up the aisle, she managed to spot Daniel, who was sitting on the groom's side, watching her, video camera in hand. Daniel's offer of help had come in handy when Kathryn's previous video support fell through. It also kept Kathryn from having any sort of not-bride bridezilla moment, something Shelby and everyone else was grateful for.

Damn, he looks good, Shelby thought as she walked past him, smiling. She felt like the most blessed girl in the world. After her conversation with Kathryn, she felt more certain than ever before that moving forward with Daniel was what she wanted. She didn't care if dating for a little less than two months was too soon—she knew in her heart that he was the one for her. All the synchronicities and the visits from his mother only further supported what she felt was true in every cell of her body, mind, and spirit.

Shelby snapped back to reality as Kathryn walked down the aisle. She couldn't believe how stunning Kathryn looked, her champagne lace fitted gown hugging her slender body in all the right ways. She looked over at and Jess and Audrey who were doing their best to fight back tears. Tears poured down Scott's face as he watched Kathryn come toward him as Gavin DeGraw's "Follow Through" played softly in the background.

Shelby looked around, as many of those in attendance also wiped away tears. And it wasn't solely from the sight of Kathryn or even the tenderness of the loving lyrics. There was an energy enveloping all of them. Shelby felt the hairs on her arms and on the back of her neck stand on end as goosebumps covered her. Just then, a slight breeze blew through the garden. Shelby made eye contact with Daniel. Something was brewing…and she was sure Daniel could feel it as well.

"Kathryn and Scott have asked you all to be here today to join with them in this beautiful ritual to co-create their life together," said the officiant, a woman in her mid-forties with long, flowing, amber locks and a form-fitting navy dress that made her look like a goddess sent from another world. "Each of you has offered something meaningful to the lives of

Kathryn and Scott, and so you are here to bear witness and hold space for their loving union."

The officiant paused, and Kathryn and Scott squeezed one another's hands tightly, both of them now with tears streaming down their faces. Kathryn leaned in, placing her hand on Scott's face, kissed him, and whispered, "I love you."

Shelby felt her eyes well up with tears. The love between them was so heartfelt, it was impossible not to join them in this expression. She looked out into the audience and noticed that everyone was riveted and feeling the intensity of love and emotion between Kathryn and Scott.

The breeze picked up again and the officiant raised her hand to offer a blessing.

"We call on Mother, Father, Earth, Gaia, God, Goddess, Loved, and Lover to bless this union between Kathryn and Scott." The wind picked up, blowing the woman's amber locks behind her as Kathryn and Scott moved in closer together to hold one another, their arms wrapped around each other's waists. "May their love cover the far corners of the earth and may its blessings reach all with whom they come into contact. May they truly know love as it has been created and may that love set them free. May all the elements surround Kathryn and Scott, supporting their love journey together, and may the heavens and all the physical and non-physical beings in it and here on earth, join together to show their love and support for this union."

The wind blew with a forceful gust, leaving behind a soft whistle that sounded a lot like an "Amen" from beyond. The audience must have picked up on this as well, as everyone instinctively replied with an "Amen."

Before she knew it, tears also fell down Shelby's face, while chills covered her entire body. She could feel the energies around them—it was as if they were all standing in a circle around Kathryn, Scott, the officiant, Shelby, Jess, Audrey, William and the other two not-groomsmen groomsmen. She glanced briefly over at Daniel, who sat motionless, his mouth slightly open in what Shelby assumed was awe.

Kathryn and Scott looked at one another, pressing their foreheads together, noses touching, their faces beaming.

"And so it is. Your loved ones, in physical and non-physical form, are here with us today to offer their unified blessing for this sacred union."

By the time Kathryn and Scott spoke their vows to one another, there was not a dry eye in the garden. Shelby was overcome with emotion, as much as she teased Kathryn about her not-wedding wedding, it was only now that she fully understood what Kathryn had been trying to tell her all along. The vibration was so high, the non-physical support, along with all of their loved ones in physical form supporting them, that Shelby now understood why it could not have been a traditional wedding.

The love between Kathryn and Scott was not only of this world. It was of lifetimes and it was a love that would go on forever, no matter what the outcome, extending even beyond their current lives. This was not something a legal document could contain. It was not something a government could reign over. It was beyond pen to paper—it was eternal love.

Daniel was astounded at the commitment ceremony happening before him. Shelby looked stunning standing beside her closest friend, and the garden seemed to be vibrating with such powerful energy ever since the woman with the amber hair began presiding over it.

Around the time when Kathryn and Scott were reciting their vows, Daniel felt a hand on his shoulder. He looked up suddenly, but no one was there. He closed his eyes and heard his mother's voice.

Beautiful ceremony, isn't it? It's time that the union between two souls be honored at the level it is deserving of.

Daniel smiled. She was always so eloquent with the way she spoke. She continued.

You know that this is next for you and Shelby, don't you Daniel?

Daniel inadvertently looked up. She wasn't anywhere to be

seen, but her voice and touch was so strong, it felt as though she was right there with him.

While in man-made time, you and Shelby have not been together long, you have, in truth, been together for many lifetimes, which is why it feels so natural to move in together even now. Do not worry about what others think or say Daniel. Honor what is in your heart.

Daniel took a deep breath. While he had always felt he would someday commit his life to another, he was never fully certain of what that would look like for him.

Haven't you found it odd that your writing soared from the week of the writers' conference, where you met Shelby? And then from the very minute you met Shelby, everything in your life has expanded? Your confidence increased, your writing flowed, even money has been coming to you effortlessly since she entered your life. The Universe is always communicating with you, Daniel. We, those of us on the other side, are always communicating with you, Daniel. Shelby is your destiny point.

Daniel felt her hand move from his shoulder and a cold breeze rushed past his right ear. She had left for now. His attention focused back in on the ceremony as he saw Shelby glancing his way. He wanted to smile or offer some type of expression, but he was too stunned to move.

―――

Daniel was waiting for Shelby with two glasses of red wine once she finished her not-wedding wedding photo duties. As she came walking up to him, a huge smile on her face, dressed in her candy pink strapless A-line bridesmaid dress, Daniel couldn't help but shake his head in disbelief. If someone had told him his life would consist of communication from his deceased mother and a gorgeous woman that he was in all likelihood going to spend the rest of his life with, he would have laughed in their face. But, here he was. And it was real.

"Thank you *so* much Daniel," Shelby said as he handed her the glass of wine. "You have no idea how ready I am to get out of these heels and dress, and just relax."

Daniel put his arm around Shelby's waist, pulling her to him. "You don't know how ready I am to get you out of those heels and that dress," he murmured in her ear.

Shelby turned to kiss him, letting her response be conveyed in her kiss.

"Hey, hey, you two, you better watch out or you'll be next!" Kathryn hollered at them as she walked past, swatting at Shelby's behind.

Daniel and Shelby looked at one another and laughed nervously. Daniel couldn't help but reflect on what his mother had shared with him during the ceremony. Shelby secretly hoped that since this was a commitment ceremony, there would not be a bouquet toss. She hurried to change the subject.

"So...what did you think?" she asked.

"Of the ceremony?" Daniel was surprised she wasn't immediately commenting on the amount of energy that enveloped the exchange.

"Yes, of the ceremony."

"Didn't you feel it? I thought for sure you were feeling it," Daniel asked.

"Feel...all the love? Absolutely. Or...the energy? It seemed to me like the officiant had a direct connection with Mother Nature and was using it to amplify the experience. Is that what you meant?"

Daniel was excited to have been so tuned in to all of the energy flowing during the ceremony, so much so he could share with Shelby his experience.

"Yes, the wind was definitely at the officiant's mercy. I couldn't believe how it seemed to blow through on cue. But, I think it was more than her only working with Mother Nature..."

The look in Daniel's eyes was mysterious and told Shelby he knew more than he was letting on.

"What? What did I miss? What happened? If you had another in-person conversation with your mom, I'm going to be so bummed that I missed it!"

"It wasn't exactly in person—I could only hear and feel her."

"You. Are. So. Lucky. What did she say? Kathryn will be so honored that she made an appearance at her commitment ceremony." Gone were the days when Shelby felt overwhelmed and uncertain about Daniel's mother's messages. Now that Daniel was open, the messages came directly to him and Shelby missed having that connection with a soul on the other side.

Daniel paused. And here was the tricky part of talking to Shelby about this. How did he let her know that she was his "destiny point and they were meant to also have a commitment ceremony or wedding even if they chose?" First, he was going to have to figure out what that even meant. He was going to need a little more time. So, he decided instead to say the first thing that popped into his mind, "She wants us to go visit her grave."

While Shelby was surprised that Daniel's mother had shown up at Kathryn and Scott's not-wedding wedding to ask for their appearance at her grave (a place she obviously did not inhabit), she trusted that if that's what the request had been, then it was what they should do. The following day, she went to meet Daniel at his place for a drive up to his mother's grave, which was located at cemetery near Washington Park.

It was a clear and much crisper November day than Kathryn and Scott's ceremony, which meant Shelby bundled up in her black Ugg boots, skinny jeans (complete with knee-high socks underneath for added warmth), and a fitted black fleece zip-up to prepare for their time outside. She wasn't sure how long they would be out there or what might occur, so she wanted to be prepared for anything.

As she pulled up to Daniel's studio, an eerie feeling came over her. Today was not a usual day and the grave visit that Daniel's mother had requested was going to be more than dropping off some flowers and a few words. Shelby didn't know what it was or what was going to happen, but she felt it distinctly inside of her—that something important was about to take place.

When she walked into Daniel's apartment, her intuition was confirmed. Daniel was dressed in a black turtleneck and dark jeans, with a wool jacket and heather gray scarf. His face was ashen. He seemed to be engrossed in re-arranging papers on his kitchen table, looking up briefly to give Shelby a strained smile when she came in.

"Daniel, what's going on? Are you okay?" Shelby walked over to him, reaching out for his hand.

He looked up, with tears in his eyes. "Shelby. There's something I didn't tell you about this visit."

"That's okay honey. You can tell me now if you want. Let's sit down." Shelby took him by the hand over to the edge of his bed.

"So…going to my mom's grave. Well, it's something I haven't done in a while."

"Oh, sweetie," Shelby was slightly confused. "That's okay. It's not like you have to go see her. She comes to you now." Shelby rubbed his back gently.

He stiffened and pulled away, speaking with an edge in his voice.

"And by a while, I mean since she passed—11 years. I haven't been there ever actually. I never even went to her funeral." Daniel put his hands to his face and his voice was muffled. "That's why I couldn't believe she was visiting me, and I wondered why she wasn't angry with me. Which is why when you told me she was proud of me, I completely shut down and dis-engaged from you. I couldn't fathom that she could feel that way about me, and I couldn't handle the intensity of the feelings I was having. I have been a coward; I couldn't face her or even pay her proper respect when she passed."

He took a deep breath in between sobs. Shelby sat still, listening intently, letting him process what he was feeling. "I didn't think it would be a big deal to go out there with you after she came to me yesterday at the ceremony. But, as we've gotten closer to this afternoon, I feel this heaviness and guilt inside of me. How could I be so unloving to my mother? My mother, who worked so tirelessly when she was alive to take care of me, and who even now when she has crossed over has been working so tirelessly to help get me back on the right track. And then you…"

His voice trailed off, followed by deep sobs. "You've been nothing but supportive and loving, even when I doubted that you were in fact getting messages from my mother. And taking you to the grave for the first time for me and for you is…more intense than I thought it would be."

Shelby sat next to him while he sobbed. She closed her eyes saying a silent prayer that he would be supported in connecting to the truth of the situation, that his mother held no grudges and that what mattered now was that he was showing his deep love and respect to her.

After a few minutes, Daniel sat up, looking over at Shelby, his eyes red and blurry. She smiled. He was still the most handsome man she had ever laid eyes on. She reached out and smoothed his hair, leaning in and kissing him softly on the cheek. "I love you Daniel."

He squeezed her hand. "I love you Shelby. Thank you for letting me get that out. Logically I know this shouldn't matter, but emotionally all of the guilt I've been feeling for so long is welling up and coming out. I don't even know what kind of state her headstone will be in. I had to call my aunt to find out approximately where it would be located."

"Thank you for sharing where you're at. I want you to know that I do not hold any judgment. I do not care about what happened in the past, all I care about is that we're right here, right now, and we're going to visit your mother's grave. We know that she can communicate with us whenever she wants and vice versa. And now we're going to visit a place that your family carved out as a location anyone could go to feel that connection—even though it exists anywhere, at any time."

Daniel wiped his face and nodded. "I totally agree, although I didn't know any of this until the past two months. I think I need to forgive myself for not being able to do this 11 years ago. In many ways, visiting today will be like a new beginning. A beginning..." Daniel turned and faced Shelby, holding both of her hands. "that I get to have with you."

Shelby leaned in again, kissing him slowly.

"So see, it's perfect."

"It is perfect," Daniel said, wrapping his arms tightly around Shelby.

"My aunt said it was near the far right corner of the cemetery," Daniel said as he and Shelby climbed out of her black Prius.

He pointed and the two began walking in that direction, hand-in-hand.

"How are you feeling Daniel?" Shelby asked.

"I actually feel lighter since sharing with you," he said, squeezing her hand. "I feel ready to visit her grave and do what I came here to do." In his other hand, Daniel held three sunflowers, his mother's favorite flower. "You cannot not smile and look at a sunflower," his mother used to say. Every time Daniel saw one, he would hear her words. Now, he could make himself and his mother smile by facing what he had long been avoiding. He didn't even know why going to his mother's grave was the first thing he said when Shelby asked about his mother's request. But, he had a sense he was about to find out.

Shelby wasn't sure what it was Daniel came there to do, but she knew she supported him wholeheartedly. She couldn't imagine being in his position, carrying around guilt and hurt for 11 years, only to realize that his mother had been with him the whole time, trying to communicate and connect with him.

As they neared the area of the cemetery where Daniel believed his mother's headstone to be, they began reading the names in search of Ann Tillman. They looked around for a bit, with no luck. Finally, Shelby said she would go further into the center of the cemetery to look while Daniel continued the search near the outside edges. She had walked several feet when she heard Daniel call out her name. His voice cracked when he tried to say more, so she knew he had found it. Shelby turned and ran back toward him. He was on his knees, brushing away grass and debris from the headstone, so he could see it clearly.

Ann Tillman

December 7, 1946 – September 7, 2002

Following bliss. Nothing ever dies and nothing ever ends. We go on forever.

Daniel and Shelby both stared at it, amazed.

"She knew all along. She never said anything to me, but maybe she knew that death was simply a transition, not a final good-bye," Daniel said.

"Which would explain why she has been trying so desperately to reach out to you for all of these years," Shelby said.

"God. I wonder how my life would have been different if I had visited this grave 11 years ago," Daniel sighed, hanging his head.

Shelby stood behind him, placing her hands on his shoulders. "Eleven years ago, you would not have been able to understand this message. You got it exactly when you needed to."

Just then, a small bird landed in front of them near the flowers Daniel had placed in a small plastic cup anchored into the grass around his mother's grave. It looked at them, moving its small beady eyes up and then down, turned, and looked out beyond the cemetery and flew off.

Daniel laughed between the tears that softly fell down his face. "Well, if that's not a sign to validate what you just said, I don't know what is." He stood up. "And now, on to what we came here to do." He looked over at Shelby and smiled, holding her hand firmly. Suddenly, he knew exactly why he had brought Shelby and himself to his mother's grave. "Shelby, you have never been properly introduced to my mother and I thought it was time to rectify that."

Shelby beamed. *He is seriously the most incredible man I've ever known. Who does this? My guy.* She thought proudly.

"Mom…I know that you knew Shelby was the girl for me

before I did. And that's why you began giving her messages. But, I wanted to introduce you to her in the proper way." Tears streamed down Daniel's face and Shelby too felt her eyes fill with tears.

"Mom, I want you to meet the love of my life, Shelby Hanson. From the moment I met her, my life has been drastically altered for the best. I am a better man for knowing her. Thank you for your persistence in showing me what I needed to see all along. Shelby *is* my destiny point." Daniel turned to Shelby.

"Shelby, I want you to meet my mom, Ann. She is, as you know, persistent, kind, loving, and, as it turns out," he said pointing to his mother's headstone. "Wise beyond what I could have ever imagined. I would not be here without her and I could not be who I am today without the both of you. And I want to ask you Shelby, will you…will you move in with me? I love you and can't wait to begin our life together."

Shelby could not contain her tears any longer, she felt overwhelmed with emotion. She and Daniel were going to be together for a very long time. And she had Ann to thank for that.

"Yes, of course," Shelby exclaimed through tears as she wrapped her arms around Daniel's neck, kissing him repeatedly. After several minutes, she wiped her tears away, gathered herself together and faced Daniel's mother's headstone.

"Ann," Shelby said. "It is my greatest honor to meet you. I want to thank you for bringing into this world such a creative, talented, and wonderful man. A man who makes my heart sing, and who, as you told me to me so long ago, is my destiny point as well. And I am so excited to share my life with him."

Daniel's eyes widened. His mom had told Shelby that he was her destiny point all along?! He should have known. His mother had never been good at keeping secrets…

10

After Daniel's mother's words to both Shelby and Daniel were out in the open and Shelby had agreed to move in with Daniel, things moved quickly and with ease. Daniel was going about his daily business when an email appeared in his inbox featuring a home that he knew would be perfect for him and Shelby. It was located in the Sellwood neighborhood of Portland, and was a small, craftsman-style home, complete with three bedrooms, composting, a small garden, and yard. He immediately contacted the owner to request a showing. Then, he forwarded the description and photos to Shelby. She called him roughly two minutes later.

"Are you thinking what I'm thinking?" she said with great urgency.

"That this is the perfect house for us?" he responded.

"Abso-freaking-lutely. Nice work, babe! You have my a-okay to contact the owner."

"Well, actually, Shelb, I already sent the email to see if we could view it either Wednesday or Thursday this week. I hope that's okay."

"First the meditation, and now this. What am I going to do with you, Daniel?" Shelby teased.

Since their time at the cemetery with Daniel's mom, Daniel

had felt more certain than ever before that Shelby was the woman he was meant to share his life with. He found himself easily thinking about their future and was taking steps to steer them in that direction. The week prior, he had suggested they do a meditation together to visualize their perfect home and call it into their lives. He had also started a conversation about marriage, and if that was something Shelby was interested in. Her answer had surprised him, and it was something he was still trying to process.

She had paused for quite some time when he had asked her what her thoughts were on marriage. This made his heart skip a beat. They had just finished watching the movie *Sleepwalk With Me* at The McMenamins Kennedy School, and the entire film centered on the topic of whether to get married and why it was (or wasn't) important.

After a few moments of elongated silence, Shelby uncrossed her legs and turned to face him. They were the only ones left in the theater, unable to leave the cozy couch they had scored to watch the film.

"Daniel, I love you and I definitely see a future together. But, after talking with Kathryn about the not-wedding versus a wedding, and then being there for their ceremony, I feel like it's important to create a new paradigm. I don't want to sign up for marriage as it is now."

Daniel was silent, he had hoped she would have chirped with glee, "Yes!" She was sending the whole topic of marriage in another direction he hadn't considered. He had assumed that Kathryn and Scott were new age hippies making a statement. He hadn't realized their statement had a profound impact on his love.

"Daniel," Shelby placed her hand on his arm. "I don't want to drive a minivan." She laughed and Daniel smiled.

"Shelby. By no means does marriage require you to drive a minivan. I swear. Scouts honor." He held his two fingers up to show his solidarity.

"I know. But it's more than that. I don't want to cook dinner every night and not work. Or be unable to manifest the highest level of abundance I desire, because I'm a wife. And while there's nothing wrong with any of these things—even the minivan—they aren't for me. Now, I don't think you require any of these things, but what happens is that these roles of husband and wife carry a powerful energy with them. And when people enter into that union, they often end up playing out what they saw growing up as the roles of husband and wife. It's totally unconscious, but it happens all the time. I want to be part of changing that paradigm. And I think part of that is creating a whole new one that energetically doesn't carry the weight that the institution of marriage does."

"You think the institution of marriage is irreversibly flawed?

"It seems that way sometimes, yes. But I do know that change is possible. And I'm suggesting that maybe that change comes from creating a new paradigm of commitment. Either way, are we in a hurry? Is there any reason we have to figure this out now? I'm sure after we've been together a while, we'll both have a more well-rounded outlook. We can allow it to flow—and have marriage and children be part of the distant future while we enjoy the deliciousness of the now."

"I'm not in a hurry per se…but I did want to see where you were at with things, because it's certainly on my mind. When would you want to re-evaluate this?"

"How about 10 years?" Shelby said with a nervous laugh.

"Really?" Daniel didn't realize her feelings around marriage were so strong. "Cause I was thinking more like two."

"Sweetie, how about we meet up with Kathryn and Scott at some point and talk to them about it? They could maybe explain it to you in a way that made more sense. I think I'm so nervous about having this conversation with you that I'm jumbling things up."

Daniel didn't want to lie, he felt disappointed. Some part of him always thought he would get married *some day* and do the traditional thing of having a wife, having her take his name, and then bringing a few kids into the world. He didn't know what a new paradigm looked like for this. Shelby was certainly bringing in a whole new way of looking at relationships into this world.

"Honey," Shelby said leaning in to him, her face lying softly on his shoulder.

"Yes, Shelby," Daniel said.

"Is this a deal-breaker for you?" she practically whispered.

Daniel turned to face her, her beautiful green eyes looking innocently into his. What Shelby didn't know, and that he couldn't say right then, was that nothing would ever be a deal breaker when it came to her. The messages from his mother, the healing, and abundance that had occurred since she entered his life was more than enough to solidify to him that he was hers—forever. Instead, he just answered quietly, shaking his head.

"Absolutely not. We'll move forward when it feels right."

But living together did feel totally right for the two of them—in fact, it seemed to be in perfect alignment. So, when Daniel saw the email for the house, he couldn't hesitate. Everything within him said, "Go for it."

"I'll let you know as soon as I hear back from the woman, so we can go see this place, which I am now going to start calling our home."

Shelby giggled. "Have I mentioned how incredible I think you are?"

"Uh no, you haven't. Maybe you should amp that up a bit."

"Well, you're the most amazing man ever! And I intend to tell you this on a regular basis. But, in the meantime, I have to get back to slaving away here at *Hello Portland*. Don't feel sorry for me though, I just sold 10 new pieces of jewelry on Etsy and got asked to do a holiday party for one of the gals who works here. I may be a solopreneur sooner rather than later."

"Congrats Shelb! That's awesome. With our new place and the three bedrooms, you can have a room for your business and I'll have a room for mine, and then one left over for both of us and all the sexy, naughty, delicious things I plan to do to you when we get to sleep together every night. We'll just call in a new, bigger house when we start having kiddos in what— 10 years you said?"

"That sounds perfect to me! And seriously. LOVE you...and hope no one is recording this call. I'm calling from my work line."

"Let 'em do it. I've got nothing to hide." Daniel was grinning from ear to ear. "Okay love, talk soon."

Shelby was having her own acceleration of abundance since she and Daniel met. She had been making jewelry more and more, and feeling less apprehensive about sharing it with the masses—or whomever she might meet. After they did their meditation last week to connect to their perfect home, she realized it was something she could do for her jewelry business as well, and she was now focusing on visualizing her business soaring.

So far, she was having incredible results. She was even thinking about getting a booth at an upcoming holiday bazaar to see how things went. In fact, Shelby was feeling unstoppable. Her work at *Hello Portland* felt unimportant and totally out of alignment with who she was. She realized that to someone else she may have what appeared to be a dream job—and at one point, it was for her.

But now, now she was ready to step more fully into her truth; coming together with Daniel had shown her that. It meant bringing whatever was out of alignment with her life now more fully into alignment. Using her passion and creativity to design and make jewelry made her heart soar. And having a portion of the proceeds go to a domestic violence shelter allowed her heart to expand even further. She had felt very inspired to have a portion of the funds go to the Raphael House and had a call in to the director there to see how it might work. It really felt as if her entire life was coming together.

―――

The home at 1174 S.E. Commodore had pretty much everything on Daniel and Shelby's list of must-haves. Hardwood floors throughout, soothing colors in every room (mint green in the living area, a second chakra orange accent wall in the master bedroom, lovely earth tones in both of the additional bedrooms, and lavender in the bathroom), a nice-sized yard with a garden plot, and a kitchen big enough for both of them to cook in comfortably.

"Oh, and it's large enough to have friends over—Kathryn and Scott are going to love this place!" Shelby said, grinning widely as she walked through the living room.

Daniel grabbed her hand and took her into the bedroom. "And with this level of support from the Universe," he said pointing to the orange accent wall. "There's going to be a lot of second chakra sexual activity happening in this room."

Shelby put her arms around Daniel's neck. "It's perfect. I cannot believe it just landed in your inbox."

"Or can you?" He said slyly, as he leaned in for a kiss. "It's sort of how we roll now, staying in the divine flow of the Universe and following the signs."

They walked hand-in-hand throughout the home, admiring the crown molding and character it embodied. The move-in timeline of three weeks was a bit tighter than they would have liked—Shelby would have to give notice and pay some overlap in rent, but overall, everything about it was a perfect fit for them.

"I normally like to take 24 hours to make a decision like this," he whispered to Shelby while the owner waited outside. "But, it feels like this is the place for us. Should we go for it?"

Daniel had never been so impulsive in his life. It had taken him years to save up the money and courage to leave his job behind to focus solely on his dream of writing full-time. And here he was about to move in with a woman for the first time in less than three weeks, after only spending a half hour in the home. He could hardly recognize himself, but at the same time, he knew to his core that he was on the right path.

Shelby hesitated in answering. Inside, she felt a "yes!", but she also had never made a decision so quickly before. She usually took time to at least speak to Kathryn or Laney about it. She sighed, looking up at him.

"Too fast?" Daniel asked.

"Too perfect." Shelby answered. "Seriously, all of this is happening so quickly and it all feels right, but my mind is having trouble keeping up." Shelby rubbed her temples and closed her eyes. "My heart is saying yes and my mind is saying, 'what are you doing?' Make sense?"

"Absolutely," Daniel said, rubbing her shoulders. "The battle of the head versus the heart. Right now, I feel like going with it. It's been working thus far. Why don't you take a minute and go outside, close your eyes, get centered and see what comes up?"

"That's a great idea. I'll go do that."

As Shelby walked out the front door of the house, she had a strong feeling of déjà vu. Had she been there before? She steadied herself and walked out to the yard, waving to the owner. "I'm going to take a few minutes to get clear about this," she said to him.

He smiled, motioning over to his car. "I'll be over here, so let me know when you're ready." He was a peaceful man, who seemed unattached to whether they took the place or not. He seemed at ease with himself, the home, and anything that came his way.

Shelby wished she could be more like that—more at ease and certain. She doubted herself far too much, especially in a situation like this. She wanted to believe people could fall in love, leap, and the Universe would totally support them. And so far, it had. But moving in together so quickly, and into a place that seemed absolutely perfect for them, was slightly (if not totally) unimaginable. Her overwhelm was coming on stronger than before, as her mind worked frantically to keep up with the rate at which she was manifesting. Shelby had heard of this happening before—manifesting so quickly that one's mind is unable to maintain pace with all of the goodness coming in. So, in an effort to feel better, the mind has to do something, anything, to get back into a more comfortable place.

As Shelby sat down cross-legged on the lawn, she realized that more comfortable place was often in her own sheltered space, not in togetherness. Yet, as she reflected on her life, time and time again she would make decisions that would keep her in that comfortable, safe space. Being with Daniel certainly felt comfortable and safe, but living together and really diving into their partnership made it all the more real. She was really doing this.

Shelby closed her eyes and took a deep breath. She quietly called in her guides and angels of the highest light, asking them for a message. Was this the home she and Daniel were meant to be in? Was it okay for them to move in together this quickly? She took several more deep breaths and, as her mind focused in on the chirping of the birds, she heard, "Yes." It came through breathy and soft, but a yes all the same. Shelby felt her heart open up a bit more and she relaxed into that space. Slowly she opened her eyes, looking out at the other houses around her. They seemed familiar, and the feeling of déjà vu returned. She was home.

Daniel walked through the house again on his own, taking it all in. He felt joy fill his heart as he imagined him and Shelby making a life together in the home. When he walked into the pale blue room, he thought he heard children laughing, catching him off guard. He knew he and Shelby had joked about having children someday (like 10 years someday), but wasn't certain how or what that would look like. He had toyed with adopting, but it wasn't something he and Shelby had spoken about extensively. He shook his head and kept walking. Something about the house was oddly familiar, although he couldn't quite place it.

He walked back into the living room and took a peak at Shelby. She was sitting out in the grass, so peaceful, the breeze slightly blowing her hair. He took a deep breath, realizing how much he loved her and how much he trusted whatever outcome came in for her. He felt the house was theirs and, while he hoped she did as well, he knew that in order to move forward, they both had to be fully in agreement—which showed they were aligned on their path together. Otherwise, they would be working uphill and that never worked—for anyone. Going with the flow was the only way to proceed.

Daniel stood in the center of the living room, closing his eyes, noticing that tears were now filling them. He felt his heart chakra expand, and he knew. This was their home.

Shelby interrupted the quiet, "Daniel, let's do this. This is our home."

The next two weeks were a whirlwind, as Daniel and Shelby made the necessary arrangements to fully claim their new home, while letting go of their current residences. Shelby was managing this in the middle of increased orders for her jewelry line, while juggling her job at *Hello Portland*. Daniel found it effortless to let his studio go, but noticed that when he wasn't able to write, he became more easily irritated and frustrated. He found himself beginning to focus on what wasn't working—no word from Jonathan or any agents/publishers he had sent the manuscript to, and lag time in receiving payment from *The Sun*, a magazine he had recently written for.

"Shelby," Daniel said one night after they had spent several hours packing up boxes at her place. "I think I need to have some energy work done. I'm cranky and definitely not in the flow like I want to be. Have you noticed that too?"

Shelby brought Daniel a glass of sparkling water with lime in it and stroked his hair gently. Tilting her head to one side, she said rather seriously, "I've noticed you curse a lot more when you're packing boxes, yes."

Daniel took a long drink, trying to contain his grin. "Well, that's one way of answering the question," he said poking her lightly in the side. "But really, are you feeling like you need energy work at all? Cause I think I definitely need my energy field balanced and whatever else they can do to me."

"Surprisingly, I'm doing okay. It's a lot to juggle, but I feel so excited about what's happening with us and with my little side business growing, it's all okay. What kind of energy work are you thinking?"

"I've had a couple of BodyTalk sessions in the past with this delightful British woman and I feel like contacting her for another one. When I was at the beach in Maui after you left, I got a sign from my mom that I should schedule a session with her and that she could support me with all of these transitions. It feels like I'm definitely overdue for a session. It seems like it will get me away from focusing on what's not working, and back aligned to where you are—in seeing all the good that is happening for us with this move."

Shelby nodded, suddenly inspired to shift Daniel's energy on her own. "That's awesome honey. I love how your mom was guiding you to receive energy work because she knew these transitions with us were going to happen. And in the meantime…" Shelby said, as she put on her best seductive smile, playfully raising her right eyebrow. "Let's shift some of that downtrodden energy with a little energy work by Shelby." She then gabbed Daniel's glass of sparkling water, took a long sip, and led him into her mainly packed up bedroom.

It was t-minus two days until move-in when Daniel went to see Gabby Adison, a BodyTalk practitioner and intuitive healer with a thriving practice and lovely healing space in Multnomah Village. While everything had come together extraordinarily well with the move, Daniel still noticed his tendency to get irritated about little inconveniences and his almost addictive email checking to see if he had heard from anyone about his novel. After continuous checking on his payment from *The Sun*, it finally appeared, but not without too many stressful thoughts about money and how everything was going to come together. Daniel needed to re-center and he hoped that's exactly what his session with Gabby would bring.

Gabby was in her late forties with flowing blonde hair, effervescent blue eyes, and an English accent that held all her American clients captive. She had been practicing BodyTalk since it was developed in 1999, after spending many years as a physical therapist and yoga instructor. With BodyTalk, Gabby used muscle testing to tap into Daniel's deeper wisdom to find out what systems in his body needed to be balanced and harmonized for his highest health and good. For Daniel, it was an opportunity to commune with his deeper wisdom and find out what the messages were in his increased irritability and hyper-vigilance around finances and his career—especially since it had gone into such a state of flow and abundance since meeting Shelby.

As Daniel lay on the table, surrounded by candles and a soft beige blanket, Gabby's soothing voice and the healing energy of BodyTalk began to sink into his consciousness. Soon, he felt like he was floating.

"We're releasing a fear of not making it in the world, while balancing your adrenals and pituitary." Gabby tapped lightly over his head and chest, and while he could hear her words perfectly, he felt like she was far away as he drifted in and out of a sea of consciousness. He saw the ocean and smelled it, too.

"Daniel, is your mother passed on?" Gabby inquired.

This brought Daniel back to the table, with Gabby's voice coming in more strongly. "Yes, she passed on 11 years ago."

"Yes, we are balancing her to a package with Shelby and your heart—both physically and energetically—as well as the belief system that you have to do everything perfectly for it to be a success."

Daniel felt as though he were being hugged from behind, as energy began to move all around his chest and upper back. The hairs on his neck and arms rose as he felt a cool breeze brush over him.

"Gabby, do...do you feel that?"

She patted him lightly on the shoulder. "Just breathe into whatever you're feeling Daniel. Trust it."

With those soothing words, Daniel drifted up and out again, floating as Gabby continued the session. In what seemed like only minutes later, she patted him again on the shoulder, whispering that she wanted him to lie there for another 5 minutes or so while the healing formula downloaded. She would come back in with some water after that and he could get up.

After Gabby left, Daniel continued to feel movement in various parts of his body. A lot of activity was happening in his heart, and he also felt movement down at his feet. He focused on breathing into whatever area of his body became activated—remembering Gabby's words to trust what was taking place. At one point, he thought he saw his mother, like a wispy figure, floating along with him. But as soon as he noticed it, his conscious mind kicked in and she vanished.

Shortly after, Gabby returned.

"How are you feeling Daniel?"

"Light, like I was floating most of the time. And my mom—she showed up briefly, but once my mind recognized her, she was gone." Daniel sat up on the table and Gabby handed him a glass of water. He hadn't noticed it until then, but he was dying of thirst. He quickly gulped down the water as Gabby stood across from him watching. "You know what's weird? My mom was sending me and Shelby lots of messages, but since we visited her head stone, she's been totally quiet. It's strange…but when I saw her, I got the impression that she was moving on to something else, although I'm not sure what. Maybe her next life…" Daniel's voice trailed off as his rational mind attempted to make sense of his vision and the message that was being transmitted to him.

"Go easy Daniel. We moved a lot of energy for you. Keep drinking water—you'll want to stay well hydrated while this healing is integrating more fully into your consciousness. Can you rest after this?"

Daniel looked over at her, noticing how the colors in the room, which seemed muted when he came in, were now more vibrant. The blue and green hues popped out and Gabby's yellow tunic seemed much brighter than before. It was like he was seeing with new eyes.

"I think I might be able to squeeze in a nap. We're moving in two days, so it's kind of go-time right now. But, I do feel like

I need to sleep for a few hours."

Gabby took the now empty glass from Daniel. "Honor whatever it is that your body needs. When you do this, you'll be surprised about how easily things flow. We tend to think we need to work harder to make things happen. What we don't realize is that all we have to do is *be* more of the time and let the Universe do the rest."

Daniel nodded. "Well, I wanted more flow, so I will follow your advice and do whatever my body asks for."

He got off the table, having to steady himself a bit and gave Gabby a big hug. Right now, he felt so in alignment, there wasn't a doubt or a worry in his mind.

Two hours later, Daniel awoke to the sound of his phone chiming. Rubbing his eyes, he couldn't believe how long and hard he had slept. He picked up his phone to discover several messages. One was from Jonathan and another from Shelby. He hadn't heard from Jonathan since Hawaii and was immediately curious. Opening up the email, he found the following:

Daniel,

It was such a joy to connect with you and Shelby in Maui, even amidst such unusual circumstances.

I've had a chance to read your manuscript and share it with a few other editors here. We really love it and would like to discuss publishing your novel. Do you have time for a phone discussion about this tomorrow around 1 p.m. PST/4 p.m. EST?

Look forward to working with you further.

Warmly,

Jonathan

Daniel blinked, rubbing his eyes and reading the message again.

He was moving in with the love of his life this week, and was potentially being offered a publishing contract.

"Damn. That BodyTalk is good," he murmured as he dialed Shelby's number.

Moving day came without incident, and as Daniel and Shelby unloaded the last few items from the moving truck, they couldn't help but burst into laughter.

"Can you believe this is our life?" Shelby said as she carried a box into the bathroom (complete with an above-the-counter bronze sink bowl).

"It's pretty ridiculous," Daniel said as he set down the last box filled with books for the living room.

Shelby galloped down the hallway and into the living room.

"You have a book deal! We live in this amazing house! My jewelry biz is booming!"

"And you'll be giving notice at *Hello Portland* soon," Daniel added.

They both found themselves, despite feeling physically exhausted, overcome with excitement, combined with disbelief over the past two days.

Daniel's call with Jonathan had been effortless. They were offering him a three-book deal over the next three years, with a generous advance, royalties, and marketing support. With one manuscript done and another almost complete, Daniel felt absolutely confident in his ability to meet his end of the contract, and attend book signings and other events to support his marketing efforts. He also felt very drawn to enlist the help of social media, running Facebook and Twitter campaigns. Jonathan would be sending the contract to him later in the week, for him to review with his lawyer (which Daniel was going to have to get), so they could finalize all the details and sign on the dotted line.

Daniel felt he was living part-dream, part-reality. It had taken some time for the reality of Shelby and his union to integrate fully into his mind, and he had a feeling his book deal would be the same. Ever since his BodyTalk session with Gabby, he felt more in the flow than ever before. He had made sure that he listened carefully to his body and did as it asked, especially after receiving the email from Jonathan. The

Universe knew what it was doing. And he wasn't about to mess it up.

Shelby disappeared into the kitchen while Daniel surveyed the scene. There were boxes everywhere, but soon things would be in order. Kathryn and Scott had been there earlier in the day to help them move the big stuff—Daniel and Scott had gotten the bed and couch into the house, while the ladies worked on directing their efforts. They had the next few days to begin the unpacking process and had both agreed they would not rest until the house was in a state of order. A perk of being a neat freak, Daniel surmised.

"I know we said we wouldn't rest until the house was all put together, but I believe a momentary celebration and toast is in order," Shelby said as she came back into the living room with a bottle of champagne in hand.

Daniel smiled, he loved how she made everything in life more fun. He took the bottle, while she went back in for the glasses.

"We can still work while drinking champagne. I am not opposed to that at all," Daniel called back after her.

As he popped the bubbly, Shelby beamed. "We manifest very well together Mr. Tillman."

"Indeed we do," Daniel replied, pouring the champagne in her glass. "Mom would be very proud of us."

"For finally listening to her, yes." Shelby said. Then, she said thoughtfully, "She hasn't been around lately—have you noticed that?"

"You know, I did notice. During my session with Gabby, I realized that we hadn't heard anything from her since we visited her grave site."

"Maybe she's moving on now that she got us on our path together?" Shelby asked.

"Yeah, sort of like she did her job for us and now she needs to focus on her. That's what I was thinking, too. Maybe she's getting ready to incarnate into another life. We'll have to pay attention to who amongst our friends ends up pregnant next! I'll miss her visits, not the in-person ones, of course,"

Daniel said with a chuckle. "But, I know we can call on her whenever we need her."

"Cheers to that," Shelby said.

Daniel smiled and raised his glass, adding a toast of his own. "To us and our new life together. To my mother who made it all possible. And finally, to the Universe. May it continue to bless us as we continue to follow the signs it sends."

11

Daniel and Shelby had been living in their new home for a little over a month, when Shelby noticed it. She was sitting in the living room working on a new line of jewelry to promote for the New Year when it dawned on her—she hadn't had her period that month. Suddenly her cozy blue sofa didn't feel so cozy. She had to check a calendar—right away.

"Daniel..." Shelby called out as she scurried from the living room to his office, her socks causing her to slide as she rounded the corner. Their pseudo-Christmas tree, a rosemary bush, still had lights on it, giving the house a warm, cozy glow.

"Whoa Shelb, you in some kind of hurry?"

"Must. See. Calendar." Shelby feigned dramatic, but a knot was rising in her stomach. How long had it been? Daniel had a huge wall calendar that he used to stay on track with the timeline that Penguin had outlined for his three novels. She squinted down to see the previous month. She had started on November 15—it was now nearly New Year's. Shelby shook her head.

Daniel leaned in, noticing how concerned she was.

"What's going on baby?" He asked as he rubbed her back.

She looked at him, her face red. Her mind was doing its analytical dance, calculating days/numbers, probability of actually being pregnant, etc. All she could think of was, I have to talk to Kathryn. With that, she and her sliding socks ran back out to the living room where she promptly picked up her phone and called Kathryn.

"You sure everything's okay?" Daniel called out after her.

"Mmm-hmm..." was all Shelby could muster. She didn't want to outright lie to him, but this situation was going to need a girl intervention before she even broached the topic with Daniel. They both wanted children...in the future. The fact that she was more than 11 days late gave her a shocking wake-up call. She was definitely not ready to have a baby.

The phone rang and rang, and just when Shelby was sure she was getting exiled to voicemail, Kathryn picked up the phone.

Daniel scratched his head. It wasn't like Shelby to be so dramatic and then not tell him what was going on. It was not lost on him that she hadn't *actually* answered his question. He had tried leading her with the "you sure everything's okay?", even though she had implied otherwise. Even so, Daniel was no dummy. A "mmm-hmmm" was not a legit answer. But, whatever it was clearly needed Kathryn's input before he was granted access to it. He sighed and then smiled. It was probably better that way. It was most likely some girl issue that he would be better off not knowing anything about.

Sitting back down, Daniel stared at his computer screen, his mouth slightly ajar. He had a three-book deal. Now, he had to complete his second novel and get going on the third. The problem was, he was stuck. His mind could not come up with a strong way to end the story. His characters had faced their conflict and had come back to a place of peace. The fact that he had people waiting to read this novel was adding to the pressure. What if his first novel was a fluke and they hated his next two books?

Not helpful self-talk, Daniel. Re-frame, re-frame.

Daniel took a few deep breaths and began tapping Cortices,

it calmed him down tremendously, allowing him to relax and refocus. Besides, he wasn't going to get anywhere if he worried about what Jonathan or Penguin thought about his work.

Didn't he know that none of his writing came from his mind, but rather from his soul? Why he had spent the past few hours trying to mentally make it happen was beyond him. Sometimes, he forgot that everything he needed was already inside of him. So, he closed his eyes, breathing into his characters and their souls. Then, he placed his hands over his keyboard.

And began to type.

———

Shelby had tried to tell Daniel she was leaving, but he was so engrossed in his writing, she decided not to disturb him. Besides, she figured the less dramatic she was about where she was going and what she was doing with Kathryn, the better. So, she wrote him a quick note and scurried out the front door.

She was meeting Kathryn for tea at Jade Patisserie in Sellwood, known for its gluten-free offerings and off-the-charts delicious macaroons. And right now, Shelby felt like she needed about 20 of the white chocolate sea salt macaroons. A sugar-rush was sure to dissolve the terror of actually being pregnant.

But, the macaroon food fest was going to have to wait. From the moment she walked in the door at Jade, Kathryn was all business.

"Okay, how many days late are you?" were the first words out of her mouth.

Shelby looked around, a bit exasperated. She leaned over the table and said in a high-pitch whisper, "Geesh Kathryn, why don't you let all of southeast Portland know that I'm a little over 11 days late for my period."

"11 days. Okay. Alright. I was 11 days late once...you're probably fine."

"Um, were you having sex?"

Kathryn rolled her eyes. "Semantics. No, I wasn't. But, my

point is—it happens. You're probably fine. Besides, nothing ever happens unless it's meant to happen. You and Daniel want kids, right?"

"Yes, we do. But not four months into our relationship."

"Have you had any slips as it were?" Kathryn was not wasting any time in getting to the heart of what was really going on.

"Easy killer," Shelby replied standing up. "We'll get to the details soon enough. But right now, I'm starved."

Kathryn smirked.

"I haven't eaten lunch," Shelby snapped back. As she walked over to the counter, she couldn't help but begin to add things up—she was starved, and she *had* eaten lunch, and she just snapped at her closest friend after she had raced down to meet her to discuss the possible pregnancy disaster. She shook her head; this was not looking good.

And Kathryn had every right to ask about slips. It had happened right after they moved into their new home. They hadn't yet hung up the very large mirror that was now in the living room, and Daniel had come up with a fantastic idea of moving the mirror into the bedroom. The whole "slip" spiraled from there.

Shelby hadn't been incredibly excited to make love in front of a mirror. She was worried she would end up more fixated on the possibility of Daniel looking at her cellulite, taking her completely out of the moment. But, with dimmed lights and candles scattered throughout the room, Shelby saw herself in a whole new light—literally.

Daniel walked up behind Shelby, wrapping his arms around her. "You're a goddess," he whispered into her ear.

Their naked bodies pressed against one another, as Daniel rubbed his strong, smooth body against Shelby's. The candlelight, and Daniel draped around her, made Shelby feel like she was, in fact, a goddess. The two of them, standing there like that, feeling one another and looking into each other's eyes through the mirror was more erotic than Shelby could have imagined.

Pleasure filled her body as she arched her back into Daniel. He covered her neck with kisses, letting his hands linger down to her heat, stroking her gently. Shelby was so overcome with passion, she couldn't contain herself. She turned around to Daniel and pushed him onto the bed. Their kissing and stroking reached a fever pitch and Shelby couldn't stop herself. And neither could Daniel. Sitting on top of Daniel, their two bodies in total one-ness and union, Shelby felt the depth of their connection—the passion, the emotion, the sacredness of their love. She felt so safe and so free with him in that moment, nothing else seemed to matter.

Maybe it had been the new atmosphere, the warm glow of the candles, or the intoxication of seeing their two naked bodies together through the image of the mirror, but neither Shelby nor Daniel gave a thought to using a condom that night.

"Really?" Kathryn was riveted by her story. "You were so overcome with passion that you forgot to use a condom?" she asked in disbelief. "I've never known you to be so overcome by anything. I'm quite impressed."

Shelby's head was down, her hands in her hair. "I know, right? I blame the mirror though. If I hadn't seen how hot it all was, I most likely would have had enough working brain cells to get protection. Damn mirror," she said, shaking her head.

"Okay, even so, it is truly a miracle every time a woman gets pregnant. So, just because you had a mirror incident—and sweetie, it happens to the best of us—doesn't mean you're with child. It's probably nothing. You moved in together, we just wrapped up the holidays, you've been under a lot of stress. That's all it is."

Shelby grabbed another macaroon.

"You know what you need?" Kathryn asked.

"A new, baby-less uterus?" Shelby inquired.

"A pregnancy test."

―――――

Daniel emerged from his writing room, only to find the house dark and quiet. He had gone into such a writing zone, he wasn't sure how much time had passed or where Shelby was. He walked through the house until he found a note on the fridge from Shelby saying she was going out to have tea with Kathryn. He peaked into the living room, to discover that Shelby had left all of her jewelry-making equipment and supplies scattered around with the television still on (she was watching the complete series of *Sex & The City* as her winter activity), the *Sex & The City* DVD intro screen shining brightly in the darkness of the house, although the volume was on mute.

"That's odd," Daniel mumbled as he turned off the television and DVD player.

It was as if Shelby ran out of the house without a thought.

As Daniel went to walk toward the bathroom, he thought he saw something move in the shadows, near the laundry room. He noticed a slight breeze tickling his skin. He caught his breath. It had been a couple of months. Could it be?

"Mom?" Daniel asked.

He thought he saw the shadow move again. Did she have a message for him?

"Mom, is everything okay?"

There was no response.

The shadow moved and Daniel followed it. It went straight into the room that was meant to be Shelby's jewelry studio, but for now housed boxes. Even so, Shelby had been more content to watch reruns of *Sex & The City* and make jewelry in the living room.

The shadow lingered for a bit in the empty bedroom and then slowly faded into nothingness. Daniel didn't understand why it wanted to hang out in the spare bedroom. He shook his head and said, "Well mom, if you decide you want to come visit us again, you're always welcome."

———

Shelby came in shortly afterwards, her head hanging down, tears in her eyes.

"Are you ready to tell me what's going on love?" Daniel inquired. He sensed that whatever Shelby and Kathryn had discussed was now ready to be shared with him. He wanted to tell Shelby about the shadow in the spare room, but decided it would have to wait.

Shelby sighed and sat on the couch. She handed him a grocery bag.

"Well, let's start here." She said.

Daniel opened the bag, there was only one small box in it. He reached in and grabbed it.

"What the? A pregnancy test? What's going on? Do you think…?" Daniel's voice trailed off as his mind worked to calculate timeframes and unprotected sex. "The mirror…"

"Yep, that damn mirror Daniel. What were we thinking?"

"We weren't," Daniel smiled, placing his hand on Shelby's leg, rubbing it softly. "But really, that was one time and I practically pulled out."

Of course, this was not entirely true, but Shelby didn't have the energy to correct him. What was done was done. Now, it was time for them to find out if the "damn mirror"—as it was about to be forever branded—was leading them to parenthood.

"Ready to do this thing?" Shelby said, rubbing her eyes. She was tired. She and Kathryn had talked through it every which way. She had cried briefly when the reality of it came crashing in (Kathryn had made some comment about drinking apple juice spritzers on New Year's Eve and Shelby just about burst into tears.).

Now, sitting in front of Daniel, his denial clearly in place, Shelby wanted to know for sure what she was dealing with and make a decision from there. There were only a few things she was sure of at this juncture: for starters, she was not ready to be a mother. While being a mom sounded like a "fun" prospect "down the road", it was not something she was ready to dive into now. Yes, she and Daniel were in love, and yes, they even had the financial means and home to welcome a new addition. But, even though the practical aspects were in place, the emotional piece was not there.

Besides, Shelby had a long-held fantasy of making love to her partner knowing they were calling in the soul that would be their child. She wanted to be more intentional about it all. She couldn't imagine the Universe would allow a child to come into their lives before they were ready. And because she had such strong faith in the Universe, she held out hope that despite the mirror incident, she and Daniel would be able to remain childless for as many years as they wanted.

———

But Shelby's faith in the Universe was misplaced.

She didn't fully understand that before she incarnated, she agreed to certain events and people that she would come together with. Some would be for short periods of time (like workaholic Josh, a man she dated briefly, or like her maniacal editor at *Hello Portland,* who wouldn't be in her life forever), and others would be a bigger part of her life journey—people like Kathryn and Daniel and…Daniel's mother. Shelby failed to recognize that soul contracts are made long before we enter into each life, and that they must be carried out, no matter what feelings may arise in the moment.

Shelby walked out of the bathroom in disbelief.

One look at her and Daniel knew.

Shelby was pregnant.

AUTHOR'S NOTES

In May 2010, two months after my grandfather Earl passed on, and while on vacation in Maui, he appeared at the side of my bed in the middle of the night. I was so freaked out that I could barely breathe. He held my hand, calmly saying my name, in an attempt to soothe me. Much like Daniel's reaction to his mother's appearance, I screamed, asking him to leave, telling him I couldn't handle seeing him. Shortly after, he came to me in a dream, with a message that I was to deliver to my grandmother (and, no doubt, the message he wanted to deliver to me in person). He wanted her to know that he loved her and not to worry, they would be together soon.

And like Shelby's experience, my grandfather also wanted to warn my grandmother about some electrical issues at the home they had shared for more than 30 years. While my grandmother does not believe that something like this is possible, her reaction to my message from grandpa was thoughtful and kind (normally she would align this with an act of the devil and most likely hang up on me). Since that visit, grandpa makes rarer appearances to me, although I have awoken to see him in a wispy outline like described in the Rose Garden scene, doing some type of work in my energy field. He also occasionally makes appearances in healing sessions and psychic readings I have received.

Then, in December 2011, I began waking up in the mornings in a lucid dream state with messages for a male friend of mine. In these messages, I was told things that I couldn't possibly know. After much internal debate, I finally decided to share these messages with him, primarily due to the intensity in which it was insisted upon that I share with him. His mother had passed on 15 years prior, and began giving me very specific messages to him about practices he needed to follow and healing work he needed to do. While he admittedly thought I was partially crazy (and yes, even I was beginning to think so!), the information I gave him could not be denied.

Much of what she shared about him and what he needed was factual. And while he did acknowledge that the information rang true for him, ultimately, he chose not to follow the guidance and the path that she shared with him. It was shortly after this that she stopped giving me messages for him.

In May 2012, I came together with a man who was almost identical in nature to the Scott character featured in my first novel, *The Quest: A Tale of Desire & Magic*, even sharing the exact same initials as the character. On our first date, I began hearing, "Tell him I'm proud of him," over and over again until I was so irritated (we were about to kiss!) that I had to blurt out the message. His father had passed on 10 years earlier and during the first three months of our relationship, we regularly felt the cold breeze, light, and heat around us, signaling that his father was with us. I was also given guidance from his father that he had supported us in coming together, and that our relationship would be deeply healing for the both of us.

On a walk in August 2012, the opening paragraphs that you read in Chapter 1 began appearing in my consciousness. While I batted them away, asking that they return when I was actually at a computer, it came in with such urgency that I stopped walking and sent myself a text message with the opening paragraphs (I didn't have a smartphone at this time due to my sheer defiance of technological conformity!). The words came out so fast, I could barely keep up. As I continued to write this novel, things transpired much as they did for Daniel—I would close my eyes and let my fingers do what they needed to do. The characters and story essentially wrote itself. I never knew where we (me and the characters) were going, but trusted that the story that needed to be told would come through.

If you had told me any of this would happen to me a few years ago, I would have told you that you were crazy (along with the fact that I wouldn't be caught dead writing sex scenes, much less spiritual/paranormal romance novels!). But, as it turns out, there is so much more in store for us than we realize. Including that the other side is consistently communicating with us and doing their part to support us in fulfilling our soul purpose in our lifetime, as well as who we form partnerships with.

As I wrote this novel, passed loved ones began making more of a presence in the one-on-one sessions and healing circles I provide via my private healing practice, further confirming the power and impact our non-physical loved ones have in our lives.

What I know for sure is this: we are not alone on this journey of life. We have access to tremendous non-physical support—in finding our next true love, in our soul's purpose, in our family relationships, in claiming our abundance—and so much more. Every day can truly be a day of connection and magic, we simply need to believe it's possible.

Do you believe?

I know, I do.

xoHeather

ESPECIALLY FOR YOU...

If you would like to stay in regular communication with Heather and receive a free energetic health toolkit, sign-up here: http://bit.ly/1C7y6CR

TELL OTHERS!

Did you love this book? Has it uplifted and inspired you? Tell the world about it with an Amazon review. Reviews make all the difference especially with this level of leading edge work, and I would so appreciate your kind words. Simply go to my Amazon Author page, click on Following Bliss (or any of my other books you've read) and leave your review: http://amzn.to/1Wb8iUj

ADDITIONAL BOOKS BY HEATHER STRANG:

A Life Of Magic: An Oracle for Spirit-Led Living
http://amzn.to/1XL7jYu

A Life of Magic contains powerful, life-transforming transmissions from the JOGs – 5 non-physical guides that author Heather Strang was "introduced" to while at the John of God Casa in Brazil in 2013. The JOGs guided Heather to specifically create A Life of Magic as an Oracle so that more individuals can benefit from this Higher Consciousness perspective on living a truly magical and abundant Spirit-Led Life.

With this Oracle as your guide, you will no longer struggle or suffer to find the clarity you seek in your business, in your relationships, with money and in all areas of your life. Simply follow the practices outlined in this guide to be able to receive the answers to your questions in the Highest Light and with much ease.

After working with this Oracle, you'll receive:
- More clarity about what decisions to make in your life.
- Answers to your most pressing questions.

- Releasing of scarcity consciousness and stepping into greater Wealth consciousness.
- Increased vitality and energy.
- More Magic in your life – synchronicities, opportunities and the "right" people showing up as you are attuned to an increased level of Magic from the transmissions in this Oracle.
- Greater connection with your own Spirit Team and Source energy.

The Quest: A Tale of Desire & Magic
http://amzn.to/1Ngr4E4

Think True Love & Spirituality can't be hot?

For 30-year-old Kathryn Casey, merging the two has developed into a lifelong quest. A mind-blowing psychic prophecy sends Kathryn on a journey that melds meditation and wine, the Amazon and New Zealanders, hot sex and dark chocolate, and psychic healings complete with strappy sandals.

The Quest delves into the core of one woman's search for great love. This novel follows Kathryn throughout rainy Portland, OR, as she attempts to capture what she desires most, while avoiding the treacherous pitfalls of self-sabotage.

When Kathryn assumes she's found "The One" prophesized to enter her life, the Universe works tirelessly to bring her experiences and synchronicities that force her to think for herself. Along the way, she's visited by new and old friends alike who remind her that finding "The One" requires deeper insight into the self. Armed with this knowledge, Kathryn makes a shocking discovery that forces her to reconsider everything she thought to be true — from her lifelong quest to her desire to bypass motherhood.

And Then It Was You
http://amzn.to/1M9aG9K

31-year-old Allie Strauss thought she had found true love.

But when her husband of five years ends their marriage over breakfast one Thursday morning, Allie's world is turned upside down.

She is thrust into a dark night of the Soul and re-emerges with new highlights, a seriously up-leveled wardrobe and a new attitude that makes even her once skeptical self believe in the Law of Attraction.

In an unprecedented move, Allie gallivants down to the Gulf Coast away from the safety of her home and family in Oceanside, Oregon & winds up in the arms of a sexy stranger.

Allie's magical journey reminds her and all of us that when it comes to true love everyone wins – even when everything is on the line.

Made in the USA
Charleston, SC
30 June 2016